# mystery aNd mishap

LOUIE SERIES BOOK III

# mystery aNd mishap

A NOVEL

*Terry Webb*

# TERRY WEBB

Pleasant Word
A Division of WINEPRESS PUBLISHING

ISBN 13: 978-1-4141-0988-6
ISBN 10: 1-4141-0988-1
Library of Congress Catalog Card Number: 2007901765

# Dedication

To Kenneth N. Black, in Memoriam

# Table of Contents

# Acknowledgment

This third book in the Louie Lighthouse series honors Kenneth Black, the man known as "Mr. Lighthouse," because he was the principle founder of the Maine Lighthouse Museum as well as the lighthouse movement in the United States. Most of the artifacts he collected were first housed in the Shore Village Museum and are now permanently lodged at the Maine Lighthouse Museum in Rockland, Maine.

It is fitting that this story features a U.S. Merchant Cutter ship, the *Woodbury*, as Ken was a Coast Guard veteran of World War II and commander of the Coast Guard Cutter OJIBW. The U.S. Merchant Service predated the Coast Guard Service, and its trained personnel saved many shipwrecked seamen through its manned saving stations.

I wish to thank Ted Panayotoff, who gave me the photo of the *Woodbury* and loaned me a copy of his book, *All Among the Lighthouses*, by Mary Bradford Crowninshield, published in 1886. This book gave me the details for this story of how the Fresnel lens worked.

I hope that Louie, his friends and his supportive community of adults give young readers in the twenty-first century as much pleasure and appreciation for the service lighthouse keepers and their families provided as the readers of Ms. Crowinshield's book did at the beginning of the twentieth century.

# CHAPTER 1

# Mystery Flotsam

Milking a cow on an island was not an easy job, especially with frozen fingers.

"Brr!" Louie exclaimed, stomping his feet and rubbing his hands together. He stroked the cow's udder. *She must have an internal combustion machine to give off so much warm milk when it's so cold outside,* he mumbled to himself. He moved his fingers up and down, guiding the milk from the cow's teats into the pail at his feet. Scout, his Newfoundland puppy, chased her tail round and round while Louie worked. But she still kept her distance from Betsy, their lighthouse island cow, who had once given the puppy a swift kick.

Scout ran down to the water's edge. Louie glanced up to see a large mass swishing to and fro with each wave near shore. *Probably flotsam,* he thought as he turned back to the task at hand. He carried the full milk pail up their house. But Scout didn't follow. Instead, she stayed near the floating mass, barking nonstop.

"Better check it out," Ma said to Louie when he handed her the milk pail.

Louie turned around and trudged back toward the shore. "What the...?" he mumbled when he reached the floating mass. "Look's like someone's laundry caught by a wave...or...no!" Louie gasped. Two eyeballs stared up at him through the mass of swirling clothes.

Louie pulled at the clothes and an arm appeared, followed by a bloated body. He thought of dragging the waterlogged body up to higher ground, but it was too stiff and heavy and he was scared to touch it.

"Ma! Come...quick!" he yelled.

Ma came running while Scout ran round and round, barking at the lifeless form. She helped Louie pull the body up above the high-tide mark.

"Fetch a blanket, Louie," she said.

"Who...what...is it?" Louie asked when he returned with the blanket.

"Don't know," Ma answered. "But we best put up the SOS flag for the lighthouse tender. This body needs to be taken to the morgue and the next of kin notified. It should also be given a decent burial."

After covering the body with the blanket, Louie walked with Ma back up the hill to the Two Tree Island Lighthouse and helped her raise the SOS flag.

# CHAPTER 2

# Looking Back

Many weeks had passed since Charlie, Louie's best friend, had gone back home with Charlie's mother and brother, Ben, on the U.S. Merchant Revenue Cutter *Woodbury*.

Charlie had come to stay with Louie after his father's fishing boat went down in a hurricane off the coast of Nova Scotia, while Charlie's mother had gone to stay with Ben, who had survived the storm.

Louie had spotted the smokestack of the ship through the spyglass while he and Charlie were cleaning the windows in the lighthouse tower. At first they both thought the cutter was just another ship heading for port. Louie remembered commenting on her low, sleek lines and two masts.

"Look, Charlie," he said that day, handing the spyglass to Charlie. "She's headed this way."

"Wonder where she's from?" Charlie replied.

"Can you see her name?"

Charlie studied the ship. "*Wood…bury.*"

The two took turns watching through the spyglass as the cutter drew closer to Two Tree Island and anchored.

"Let's go tell Ma and try to raise their attention to make sure they row their dory in down to the new landing area I built," Louie said.

Both boys raced to the shore with Scout at their heels. The dory was soon lowered from her derrick on the large ship into the water. One person was already seated in the dory. *Strange,* Louie thought. *I've never seen that before.* Three other people then climbed down a rope ladder and got into the waiting dory. When Louie and Charlie waved frantically to get the attention of the people in the dory, one person waved back.

As the dory drew closer, Charlie exclaimed, "That's my ma!"

"And I think that's Ben!" Louie added.

Louie and Charlie maneuvered the dory onto the slip and hauled her up the ramp. Charlie's brother, Ben, who was wrapped in a blanket, sat on the bow seat.

"Am I ever glad to see ye!" he exclaimed, his big grin wrinkling his cheeks. Ma, who had by this time joined them, reached her hand out to Mrs. Missen to help her out of the dory. Two crewmen grasped Ben under his armpits and gently lifted him off the seat and over the side of the boat.

Only one of Ben's legs appeared over the side. Louie waited to see if maybe his other leg was bent and he was sitting on it. But no—that pants leg only half-covered where the other leg should have been. Large bandages circled Ben's hands. Louie had to swallow a gasp, clear his throat and look away. Charlie didn't seem to notice. He threw his arms around Ben, hugged him and said in a broken voice, "I'm glad…you're back."

The two crewmen half-carried and half-walked Ben between them up to the house. Ma fixed tea and coffee with biscuits for everyone. Ben's mother then told them all that had happened to Ben's other leg.

"The doctors tried to save Ben's feet and fingers, which had suffered severe frostbite, but they were only able to get the circulation back in one foot. The other foot remained numb and cold. When gangrene set in on that leg, they had to amputate it below the knee. Almost all of Ben's fingers had to be amputated for the same reason. They could only save two—one on each hand. He has to keep the bandages on for a while longer."

"The pain's pretty awful sometimes," Ben added. "But it's not nearly as bad as it was that day I watched the *Tipsy* go down and all her crew drown. Someone must have sure as a gun been praying for me."

"Many of us have been praying," Ma added. "You survived. God must have a special plan for the rest of your life."

It was then Louie thought to himself, *But what can he do without a leg and two fingers?*

"The merchant cutter that brought us back has all kinds of life-saving gear," Ben said and then began rambling on about the *Woodbury* and her equipment. "A Lyle gun[1] and a breeches buoy[2]… The seamen got me on board in the breeches buoy when the doctors said I was ready to sail back from Nova Scotia.

"The best equipment of all is the Marconi wireless that has just been installed. I got to watch them testing it on the way here." Ben's eyes lit up as he told them about this fancy new equipment.

"How'd ye like to come aboard?" One of the life-saving crew standing nearby said to Louie and Charlie. "Afterward, I'll show ye how to work the Lyle gun."

"High tide will be in about an hour," Ma replied. "Then you can bring your ship in closer. Meanwhile, Ben can rest here."

Later, after the tide had come in, Louie and Charlie climbed aboard the ship. The captain greeted the two boys and introduced them to a man named Mr. Garçon. Mr. Garçon told Louie and Charlie that he was the representative of Signor Marconi, the famous inventor and businessman.

"Hired by the great Italian himself," Mr. Garçon told Louie after he showed them both how the wireless worked. "Soon there'll be one of these in every lighthouse and on every ship."

*How I wish!* Louie thought. *Then I could find out baseball scores as well as communicate with all my friends on the mainland.*

"You've seen history in the making, boys. Here, I'll give you some newspaper clippings about this new invention and its creator." Mr. Garçon handed Louie some papers. Louie thanked him, but he did not like Signor Marconi's choice of representatives—just one more person calling him "boy." *Anyone looking at how tall I am can tell I'm not a boy,* he thought.

When it was time to leave, members of the life-saving crew rowed Charlie and Louie back to shore so that Charlie could pack. They brought the Lyle gun back with them so they could demonstrate how to fire it to the ship for rescue.

"Maybe someday you'll set up a life-saving station right here on Two Tree Island," one of the crew said to Louie.

Charlie packed his duffel in a hurry so that he could join Louie for the Lyle gun demonstration. The life-saving crew members who had brought the two boys back to shore showed Louie how to coil the hawser rope in such a way that it would lie flat in a box and pay out free of tangles. They attached a Tally Board[3] to the line and fired the gun so that the Tally Board landed on the cutter. Louie and Charlie had tried to read the words on the board ahead of time, but it was written in French—a language neither of them understood.

Louie watched as two seamen on the *Woodbury* tied the rope to a mast above the block and then put the breeches buoy on the rope. Louie pulled on the rope to bring the buoy to shore. The seamen on the ship loosened the rope with its Tally Board and Louie, with Charlie's help and under the supervision of the life-saving experts on shore, pulled the rope to shore and coiled it into the box so that the rope would not tangle.

"Now ye've had yer first lesson in life-saving," one of the men told Louie. "We're going to leave this Lyle gun on the island. Stow it where you can get to it fast. Winter's coming, and you never know when you might need to use it."

"Here's cross hand'n ye," said Charlie to Louie, using their special communication for goodbye. He climbed into the dory with Ben and his mother and waved until the dory came alongside the cutter. Louie watched as the crew helped hoist Ben on board. He waved the cutter off as she steamed out of sight.

---

[1] A small canon, named after David Lyle. It shot a rope over to a ship from a shore position to rescue stranded seamen from sinking ships.

[2] A seat that could carry people on a hawser rope from a boat to shore.

[3] A wooden board like a paddle with words that read: "Make sure the hawser fast about two feet above the tail block. See all clear, and that the rope in the clock stays free. Then show signal to folks on shore." Instructions were written in English, French and Spanish.

# Chapter 3

# Waiting, Writing and Wondering

The sloop *Islanda* responded first to Louie's SOS. Captain Shiver saw the flag flying as he was hauling lobster traps nearby. "What's yer problem?" he hollered through his horn.

"Got an unidentified body that just washed up on shore," Louie hollered back.

"Wal, I'll be doggoned. Never know what will fetch on these shores. I'll let 'em know."

As soon as he had baited his trap, Captain Shiver headed into the harbor. Louie finished his daily chores and wrote some letters to give to the lighthouse tender or Gus the mailman, whoever arrived first. He finished the letter he had started to write to Uncle Sam. The Reverend Sam Hornblower had been like a father to him.

Dear Uncle Sam,

Ben and his ma arrived on the Merchant cutter *Woodbury*. I wish you'd been here to see her! She had all kinds of life-saving gadgets on board and one of those new wireless telegraphs. It was sweet and sad to see Ben. Seeing him alive and smiling was a real miracle—but he's lost part of a leg, one foot and most of his fingers. The crewmen had to carry him. What's he going to do? He can't even walk. Suppose he'll have a cane and even a peg leg one of these days. But he still has no fingers, so he can't write—can't fish. Charlie went back with them. You know how Charlie's always getting into trouble. Suppose he'll be expected to be the man of the family now—at least until Ben's better. Wanted to tell you all of this because you're the only one who can help Charlie and Ben—like you helped me.

—Louie

P.S. Guess what just happened? A dead human body washed up on shore near the boathouse. We don't know who it is (or was). We've covered the body and are waiting for an official to come and examine it and take it to shore for identification and burial.

—Louie, again

Louie then wrote a hurried letter to Charlie. The two friends had agreed to write each other every week. When the *Woodbury* came to fetch Charlie and his ma, neither Charlie nor Louie had wanted to leave the other. Since both were fatherless, their bond of friendship had deepened, but Charlie still held on to his raw memories.

Dear Charlie,
    Scout just found a human body washed up on shore! It's weird. We're waiting for an official to come and take the body. Don't know who it is or how it died. Wish you were here to help solve the mystery. How's Ben? How's school? Write soon.
    Here's cross hand'n ye!

—Louie

With still no sign of either the tender or Gus's mail boat, Louie reluctantly continued with his assigned lessons. Miss Gilbert had sent his assignments on the last mail delivery and had written this letter in her neat cursive writing:

Dear Louie,

Since winter is coming and I will not be able to come back to the island until spring, I'm sending you this large packet of lessons to complete. You can return the assignments to me as you finish each one. Sometime after Christmas, I'll be sending you some eighth-grade examinations to take—to see how well prepared you are and where you need to concentrate if you're still behind.

I congratulate you on your excellent paper answering my question, "What light guided Captain Mitchell's longboat?" It was thought provoking and creative.

I recently attended one of Samuel Clemens's lectures. He shared many interesting bits of wisdom. One I liked and thought you could write about is, "The man with a new idea is a crank until the idea succeeds."

I'm also enclosing some newspaper clippings about Henry Ford, who has an idea to mass-produce the horseless carriage. You might find others who have a new idea. Pick one and write an essay telling me whether you think the person's idea will succeed or not and how it will change the way we live our lives if it does.

Keep up the lessons in your Geometry book and in Buckley's *A Short History of Natural Science and the Progress of Discovery*. Prepare two reports for me. Describe in detail, with illustrations, how your Fresnel lens works to give off that powerful beam of light. Then do some research and write about a new species of life you've found on Two Tree

Island. Give its scientific name and tell about its origin, habitat and mannerisms.

Finally, I've enclosed Harriet Beecher Stowe's book, *Uncle Tom's Cabin.* Please write a book report when you've finished reading it. Tell me what you learned about slavery and its impact on the Civil War.

I will look for new mail from you within the next month.

—Miss Gilbert

Although Louie liked reading and writing poems, he didn't always like all the other subjects he had to learn. But doing lessons was better than anxiously waiting for the rescue boat to arrive and moaning about all he was missing on shore.

*Besides,* Louie thought, *doing lessons would take away from the lighthouse routine that I find boring most of the time. Like now. Milking Betsy is okay, and collecting eggs is okay—as long as I get to eat some. But bringing coal up to the house or having to keep the lighthouse beacon going all night and on foggy days are not just boring but plain exhausting. Playing with Scout and teaching her tricks—now that is fun. Finding out whose body that is down by the boathouse—now that is spooky.*

Louie found it hard to keep his mind on his assignments. He kept thinking about the body and wondering how the person drowned. *Did the person fall overboard or come from a ship wrecked in a storm? Did the person leave any children behind?*

Louie looked up from his ponderings when he heard his mother climb up the steps to enter his bedroom. "Sounds like Miss Gilbert has given you some challenging assignments," she said.

"And she remembers how much I love to write," Louie replied. He put down the book by Harriet Beecher Stowe he had been reading and joined her to light the lamp beacon and write in the logbook.

*November 15, 1903. Chill N.W. wind, 10 knots with strong gusts. Found dead human body.*

—Louie Hollander

# CHAPTER 4

# The Inspector Arrives

The hardest part of being a lighthouse keeper is not knowing…

Louie's thoughts rambled on as he went about his lighthouse chores the next morning.

He extinguished the lamp and picked up the spyglass. The wind had apparently diminished during the night, as he could no longer see whitecaps. There was no fog either, so he did not need to use the fog siren. Maybe this morning the lighthouse tender or a merchant cutter would come for the body that still lay covered near the cowshed.

Louie had seen the body every day on his way to milk Betsy. But he didn't—dared not—touch it. He had learned that much from reading detective stories. Yet this morning, he just couldn't resist peeking at it under the cover. When he did, vacant eyes stared up at him. One cheek had been bitten off, and the forehead was smashed in above one eye. The body was beginning to give off an unpleasant odor. Louie held his nose and put the covering back over the body. Scout sniffed, and her dog hairs stood up.

"I don't like smelling it either, Scout," said Louie. "Come on."

Now that they were in the tower, Scout went over to the window and put her paws up on the ledge.

"See anything out there?" Louie asked.

"Woof!" came the reply, and she wagged her tail.

Louie looked out again. Sure enough, there was a ship approaching.

"Come on, Scout." Louie hurried down the winding staircase and headed for the dock with Scout at his heels. "Ship approaching!" he shouted as he tore through the house. Ma put on her coat and joined him near the landing.

"Looks like the *Woodbury*," she said.

When the cutter neared Two Tree Island, a dory was let down and several people climbed aboard. When the dory reached the bottom of the boat slip, Louie and Ma hauled her up.

"I brought Lt. Gillespie, our assistant inspector in charge of investigations," said the captain of the *Woodbury*.

"Got a wireless message that ye have a body here needs investigating," Lt. Gillespie announced to Ma. "So Captain here fetched me right quick from the life-saving station. Where's it at?"

Louie took Lt. Gillespie and the captain over to the covered body. Lt. Gillespie turned the cover back half way. "Hard to tell features," he said. "Been dead awhile, I reckon. We'll need to take the body back to the morgue. Poor soul." Lt. Gillespie covered the body back up, and the three men lifted it into the dory.

"Did you touch the body or remove anything?" Lt. Gillespie asked Louie and Ma. Both shook their heads no.

Lt. Gillespie looked all around the shoreline. He turned and walked down the beach, picking up any flotsam he found that might be connected with the body—mostly pieces of cloth that had torn off and washed up on shore.

"Were there any wrecks of ships nearby?" Ma asked.

"Nope–least not anything we've heard about. But we'll let ye know soon as we complete our investigation." With that, Lt. Gillespie and the captain said goodbye and stepped aboard the dory. The seaman rowed the small craft, with its mysterious bundle, away toward the waiting merchant cutter.

The next ship to arrive was Gus's mail boat. The boat pulled up beside the wharf on the other side of Two Tree Island just as Louie and Ma were walking back up to the house. They stopped at the house long enough to pick up their bundle of letters and then climbed down the steps to the wharf, where they exchanged parcels of letters with Gus. "See ye, soon!" Gus said as he pulled away from the wharf and headed for the next island.

"I've got two," Louie said when he loosened the string around the envelopes. He climbed up to his loft room and flopped on the bed with Scout beside him. He turned both letters over in his hand, trying to guess who they were from. "Bet this one's from Charlie," he said. "Looks like his handwriting."

Dear Louie,

Thought I'd write you from the ship so I could give it to the mail ship when we got to port. Being on this cutter is like being on a warship with all its equipment—even guns. Ben is plumb worn out from the travel and sleeps most of the time. Don't think he'll be much good until his wounds heal.

Here's cross hand'n ye.

—Charlie

Louie stared at the handwriting on the other envelope. Could it be? He opened the letter and read the scrawling signature first—Louisa Ann Peabody—the girl he had gotten to know riding on the steamer and train to attend the First World Series games in Boston.

Louie held the letter in his hand and turned it over and over gently before he read it.

> Dear Louie,
>
> How are you? I did get your postcard and haven't forgotten about you. It must have been exciting to see those first World Series games. When the Pilgrims won, Boston went wild. Did Charlie's arm get healed?
>
> I'm going home for Thanksgiving. What are you doing?
>
> Write soon.
>
> —Louisa

*Thanksgiving.* Louie hadn't thought much about it before now. Holidays were just more days to keep the lamp lit in the lighthouse tower.

At that moment, Ma called from downstairs. "The Bowlines have invited us to come to the mainland for the community Thanksgiving events and to have dinner at their house," she said.

"Yeah, Ma! But if we go, who's going to tend the lighthouse? A ghost?"

"Captain Bowline is bringing Aussie out to relieve us so we can have a few days on shore to enjoy the festivities. We'll need to stock up on supplies while we're on shore before winter hits."

"Weather permitting, of course," they both said in unison.

That night, Louie prayed for good weather for the rest of that week.

# CHAPTER 5

# Gathering in Gratitude

L ouie leapt out of bed.
He looked out his window and watched the bright yellow ball poke its head up over the horizon. "Ma!" he called downstairs. "Look! No fog and not much wind."

"Guess we should expect the *Rainbow* sometime soon," she called back.

Louie hurried to do his morning chores so that he would have time to pack his duffel. He milked Betsy, gathered up two eggs for their breakfast and brought them to Ma in the kitchen. Ma seemed not to notice. She was concentrating on writing down the list of items they would need to purchase at Jake's store.

"Oh…Louie," she said when Louie tapped her on the shoulder. "It's you. I'll cook us some of those eggs while you bring in the coal for the stove. Must remember to make some of that sea moss pudding[1] to take to shore," she mumbled to herself. "Oh, and Louie," she added, "we best pack our things to be ready when Captain Bowline gets here."

Louie stuffed his duffel bag in jig time. He tucked *Uncle Tom's Cabin* under his arm and, with Scout following, went up to the lighthouse tower to read and watch for the *Rainbow*. But with all the excitement he couldn't concentrate, and he found himself reading the same sentence over and over again. When Scout poked her nose under his arm and made him drop the book, he gave up trying to read and took the spyglass to search one more time for any sign of ships that were approaching. At last he saw a ship in the distance. He jumped up and wound his way down the lighthouse tower steps with Scout in tow.

"She's coming!" he called out to Ma. "Get ready!"

Scout jumped into the dory as soon as he saw Aussie. "Ayuh—me friend, don't go a-knock'n me down," Aussie said. He laughed his deep throat laugh and scratched Scout behind her ears. "Are ye goin' to leave her to keep me company?" he asked Louie.

"Think she'd like to see her ma and siblings," said Captain Bowline, who was also in the dory. Louie was relieved that Captain Bowline had decided to bring Scout. He liked Aussie, but Scout was still his dog. He wanted his puppy to come with him.

"You'll find everything you need as ship-shape as can be," said Ma. "Thanks for coming."

Willy, Captain Bowline's eight-year-old son, was waiting for them with Scout's mother and sister when they arrived at the town wharf. The three dogs nuzzled each other with their tails going a mile a minute while Louie helped Ma and Captain Bowline unload their duffels and the food they had brought.

"Community pot luck tonight," Captain Bowline said. "Thanksgivin' service tomorrow, followed by another Thanksgivin' meal at our house. S'pect some surprise guests, too." Captain Bowline wouldn't say who the surprise guests would be. Louie could hardly wait. He tingled with anticipation.

On the way to the town landing, he told Captain Bowline all about the body he had found and how the inspector had taken it away to investigate. "Heard about it all over town," was Captain Bowline's only comment on the subject.

That evening, Louie and Willy trudged over to the town meeting hall with the Bowlines and Ma. Frost crunched under their feet, and Louie could see his breath. But he didn't feel cold. Just walking on solid level ground warmed him. He started whistling and remembering—remembering when they had gathered together at Swanton Point when Pa was still alive.

*"Over the river and through the woods…"*

The woods here were tall evergreen trees.

*"To Grandmother's house we go…"*

*Maybe there would be some grandparents there,* thought Louie. *Then it would be like family.* Sure enough, when they arrived Louie noticed there were some older adults present. He didn't know if they were anybody's grandparents, but it didn't seem to matter. Everyone appeared to be one big, happy family. He and Ma were greeted with big hugs.

"Great to see you again!"

"Louie—you must have grown three inches since summer."

*Actually,* thought Louie, *I've only grown two inches.*

Some of the old men walked with the aid of their canes. A few of the older women took the dishes that the Bowlines and Ma had brought and placed them with the others on one of the long tables. The younger men and some of the older boys were slicing the turkeys. Some of the younger boys were playing marbles in the corner. Willy joined them.

Louie noticed that most of the kids his age were gathered around the player piano in the corner. One of the girls grabbed Louie by the arm.

"Come over and see what tunes it plays," she said.

As Louie drew closer, he could hear the refrain, *"Bill Bailey, won't you please come home"* coming from the piano. The keys moved up and down, but there were no hands playing the keys. Louie leaned in closer and tried to figure out how the keys were playing by themselves.

"See those rolls?" said one of the boys. "Here's one of Stephen Foster's songs and another with Tin Pan Alley hits." They showed Louie other rolls. Louie had sung some of the songs in his old school. Soon, he was singing the lyrics with the other kids. Then a deep voice joined in the singing from behind. Louie turned to see to whom the voice belonged.

"Charlie!" Louie cried. Next to Louie stood his pal and mentor, Uncle Sam. "So this is the surprise!"

Captain Bowline grinned. "Just the beginin'," he said.

"Feast's ready for eatin'," one of the women called out.

After the parents had collected the small children and filled their plates, everyone else heaped his or her plate with roast turkey and food from the variety of side dishes. They sat around the long tables and bowed their heads while Reverend Sam Hornblower said the grace.

"We have gathered here today, as our pilgrim father did so many years ago, to thank God for our many blessings: the food we are about to share, the lives that have been spared from the ravages of storms, our families, friends and neighbors. Be present at our table, Lord, and be with us in our fellowship. Amen."

---

[1] Recipe: Ground dried moss into a powder. Put the powder into a cheesecloth in a quart of milk in a pan and bring it to boil. Take the cheesecloth out, squeezing out all the juice into the pan. Now add vanilla to taste, and let it set.

# CHAPTER 6

# Thanksgiving Day

W orship first, then more feastin'," Captain Bowline announced the next morning as they entered the white clapboard church in the center of town.

He was a man of few words, but what he said mattered.

Louie and Charlie had slept at the Bowlines the night before, camping out on the floor of Tommy's room with Scout and the other two dogs at their feet. Tommy wouldn't go to sleep until he had quizzed Louie about the body he had found and Charlie about his ride on the merchant cutter. Louie promised that the day after Thanksgiving, they would all three go sleuthing to learn what they could about any missing persons.

Louie and Charlie had talked—or whispered—late into the night after Tommy finally dozed off. "I've been trying to get caught up at school while helping Ben the best I can when I'm home," Charlie told Louie. "He was in a lot of pain when he got home. The trip tuckered him out. Ma took him to the doc, who changed the bandages on his hands. The leg—or what's left of it—is what's causing most of the pain. Doc calls it 'phantom pain.' Says it will go away in time.

"We told Ben all about the memorial service we had for Pa. Ben's taken to reading the Bible. Uncle Sam made a wooden stand for Ben so's he can read in bed. He's tryin' to get back into his school studies, too, and walkin' with a cane. Soon as the stump heals, he'll get one of those prostheses.

"Uncle Sam has come over as much as he can. When he suggested I come with him for the Thanksgiving community dinner and service here, I wasn't sure Ma would let me. But she said the neighbors had invited them for Thanksgiving and to go ahead."

When the familiar hymn began the Thanksgiving service the next morning, Louie had to cover up a yawn with the back of his hand.

*Come, ye thankful people, come, raise the song of harvest home;*
*All is safely gathered in, ere the winter storms begin.*
*God our Maker doth provide for our wants to be supplied;*
*Come to God's own temple, come, raise the song of harvest home.*

Louie didn't want to think about winter storms—just the warmth of being with his friends and family. The Bowlines and Uncle Sam were family to him now.

As Louie looked around the crowded church, he saw that Mr. McAllister had slipped into the vacant seat beside Ma during the hymn. A girl named Sally, whom he had met last night, seemed to be staring at him and smiling. Louie blushed and turned back to the hymnal in front of him.

*Even so, Lord, quickly come, bring Thy final harvest home;*
*Gather Thou Thy people in, free from sorrow, free from sin,*
*There, forever purified, in Thy garner to abide;*
*Come, with all Thine angels come, raise the glorious harvest*
  *home.*[1]

After the service, Mr. McAllister walked back to the Bowlines with Ma while Uncle Sam went with Louie, Charlie and Tommy. Louie decided that Mr. McAllister must be the other surprise guest.

While Ma helped Mrs. Bowline get their family Thanksgiving dinner ready, Louie joined Tommy, Charlie and Mr. McAllister in a game of Halma[2] while Uncle Sam showed Captain Bowline the most recent issue of the *Boston Globe*. The newspaper featured a story about the vision of the Panama Company to build a canal so that there would be a way for ships to get from the Pacific Ocean to the Atlantic Ocean without having to go around the treacherous Cape Horn.

"One of Teddy Roosevelt's wild schemes," Captain Bowline commented when he read the article.

"Too many lives lost on the first try to go through Nicaragua," added Uncle Sam.

"Chowdah ready, " announced Mrs. Bowline. "Turkey and fixin's, too."

After the grace was said, Louie wasted no time in finishing the clam chowder. When it was his turn, he passed his plate to Captain Bowline for turkey, oyster stuffing, mashed potatoes and squash.

"Now, what's this I hear about a body washin' up on Two Tree Island?" Mr. McAllister asked Ma.

Ma explained to Mr. McAllister that Louie and Scout had found the body and that the merchant cutter had brought the assistant detective from the life-saving station to pick up the body and start the investigation.

"You don't suppose…" said Charlie, putting down his fork. "I mean, did it look like…?" His face turned ashen.

"Don't think so," said Louie. "At least, I couldn't tell."

"You're thinkin' of yer pa's ship, ain't ye, son?" said Captain Bowline.

"Your pa was buried at sea, the way any Captain would have wished," said Uncle Sam. He put his arm around Charlie's shoulder.

Louie sympathized with Charlie. He remembered all the dreams he had of finding his pa dead when he had fallen down the Swanton Lighthouse steps. He guessed Charlie was having dreams about his pa drowning.

At that point in the conversation, Tommy spoke out loudly, "We're going to start shlossing tomorrow." This got everyone laughing, as what he meant to say was "sleuthing."

"Here's to our three daring detectives," said the adults as they all clinked their glasses.

---

[1] Alford, Henry, 1844.

[2] Halma (the Greek word for "jump") is an earlier version of Chinese Checkers. The game, for 2 to 4 players, was invented by Dr. Thomas Hill, a mathematician, teacher and preacher who was president of Harvard College from 1862-1868.

# CHAPTER 7

# Junior Sleuths

When do we start?" Tommy asked Louie, who was curled up under a quilt.

"It's too early," mumbled Louie as he pulled the covering over his head. He just wanted to sleep. He never got to sleep in at home. Tommy moved over to him and pulled the quilt off.

"Wake up! We're going shlessing."

"It's sleuthing," corrected Louie, poking Tommy good-naturedly in his stomach. "It means searching for clues. And the question is *where* we're going, not when."

The two older boys got dressed and joined the others at the breakfast table. Ma was going over her shopping list with Missus and Captain Bowline.

"Have to make sure we have all the provisions we need before winter weather socks us in," she said. "Can you think of anything I missed?" The other two looked carefully at her list.

"Maybe an extra pane of glass in case another lighthouse tower window breaks," said Captain Bowline. "Remember, you used the last one to replace the one that broke during the hurricane."

"And some extry cans of tuna and sardines, in case the fish ain't bitin'," his wife added. Ma scribbled these items down on her already lengthy list.

"Are ye ready to start detecting?" Captain Bowline said to the three boys.

"Yep!" Tommy replied.

"Think we'll check out the police station first," Charlie said.

"Good thinkin'," said Mr. McAllister, who had just arrived. "They might just have heard of a missing person around these parts."

Louie peered around Mr. McAllister to see if Uncle Sam had come with him.

"Oh, the Rev'd asked me to give you this," Mr. McAllister said as he handed a note to Louie's mother. He looked back over at Louie and Charlie. "Said to tell ye he'd catch up with ye later on today—had some appointments with folks wanting to get married."

Louie, Charlie and Tommy went to the police station by themselves. When they arrived, Louie asked the sergeant behind the desk, "Do you know if anyone has been reported missing?"

"Nope," the sergeant answered.

"Anybody murdered?" asked Tommy.

"Nope."

"What do you police do then all day without murders and missing persons?" asked Tommy.

"Well, now, ye see, sonny," said the sergeant, glaring at Tommy, "we git all kinds of calls at all hours—lost dogs, lost cats, lost keys—but no lost persons. Not recently, anyhow."

"But a dead body washed up on the shore at Two Tree Island," said Louie. "The merchant cutter *Woodbury* came and took it away."

The sergeant perked up. "Right tell!" he said. "Heard somethin' 'bout that. Merchant Revenue business…now run along." He brushed the three boys off and went back to writing in his police ledger.

"I've got an idea," Charlie said. "Let's try the newsstand. Maybe we'll find some clues in one of the newspapers or journals." The three detectives left the police station and headed for the newsstand.

"Got any hot news?" Louie asked the owner when they arrived.

"Like a murder?" asked Tommy.

"Or someone advertising about a lost person?" added Charlie.

"Nothin' today," replied the owner. "Just local news 'bout Thanksgivin'. Maybe in them piles of old newspapers. Yer welcome to read 'em while yer here."

The two older boys took several of the older issues of *Maine News* and the *Youth's Companion* from the pile, found a seat on a nearby bench, and began to read through them. Tommy sat at their feet and looked at the headlines and ads.

"A Brownie camera!" he cried, pointing to one ad. "If we had one of those, we could take photos of all the clues we find."

"Let's find the clues first," Louie mumbled without looking up from the paper he was reading. "Here's one…look at this: 'Overloaded steamer capsized. Still not known how many lives were lost. A week after the disaster, only 50 bodies have been recovered and identified, but there are 100 still missing, most of them women and children.'"

Louie paused from reading. "Maybe the body we found was one of those missing!"

Charlie peered over his shoulder and read the next sentence. "This accident has been called the worst human disaster to hit the Midwest in this century.'"

"Where?" said Louie. "Let me see." He took the paper from Charlie and continued reading. "Detroiters are stunned."

"Detroiters?" Both boys looked at each other. Detroit was between Lake Huron and Lake Erie.

Louie and Charlie folded up the paper and put it back in the pile. They cupped their hands on their chins and sat down to read the rest of the papers piled beside them. After an hour of scanning as many newspapers and journals as they could find that had any recent news, they gave up and started back to the Bowlines' house. Louie heard his stomach growl. *Must be time for lunch,* he thought.

When the boys got back to the house, Mrs. Bowline had some turkey sandwiches and Moxis waiting for them. "Find out anything?" she asked.

The three boys shook their heads in unison.

"No murders," Tommy said.

"Only lost bodies not found are in Lake Huron!" said Louie.

"What's your next plan?" Mrs. Bowline asked. The three boys shrugged their shoulders. "Hmm…do you suppose the Life-saving Service has found out anything?" Mrs. Bowline continued.

Charlie's eyes brightened. "I've got an idea! Let's telephone Lt. Gillespie. Didn't he take the body back to investigate?"

"Of course! Why didn't I think of that?" Louie exclaimed.

"But we don't have a telephone," said Tommy.

Mrs. Bowline thought for a moment and then said, "I think there is one at Jake's store—" Before she could finish her sentence, the three boys grabbed their coats and ran out the door.

Ma and Mr. McAllister had just finished their shopping and were loading boxes and bags onto the wagon when the boys arrived.

"Ma, can I have some money?" said Louie.

"What for?" said Ma.

"So's we can call Lt. Gillespie," Charlie answered.

Mr. McAllister handed Louie some coins. Louie took the coins and walked over to the telephone inside Jake's store. He took the earpiece off the wall mount, put in the coins and, with his mouth close to the speaker, turned the crank handle until it rang.

"Hello, can I help you?" a crackling voice answered at the other end.

"I want to talk to the Life-saving Service in Rockland," said Louie.

"Just a moment, please. I'll ring them. How's the weathah down there?"

Louie put his hand over the speaker and turned to Charlie. "She wants to know about the weather," he whispered.

"Tell her it's cold but clear," Charlie said.

Louie put his mouth back up to the speaker to answer, but when he did, he could hear someone else talking in the background through the earphone. "Hello?" he said. The two people went on talking.

Jake looked at him from behind the counter and nodded his head. "Party line," he said.

"Oh," Louie answered. He listened and waited for the operator to come back on the line. Then he heard a click-click, followed by silence.

"It's ringing!" the operator said, breaking into the silence.

"Hello?" a voice answered.

"You're connected," the operator told Louie.

"A…ah…I'm looking for…ah…" stammered Louie. His tongue wouldn't move. He couldn't remember the assistant lieutenant's name.

"Can I speak to Lt. Gillespie?" he said at last.

"Who is this?" the voice asked.

"It's Louie Hollander, sir. I'm the one who found the body on the island a while ago." Louie heard his voice echo through the line.

"I'll see if he's around," the voice answered. Tommy stood on his tiptoes on one side of Louie while Charlie craned his neck to listen to the earphone on the other. Louie put his hand over the mouthpiece. "He's trying to find him," he said to the other two.

"Hello?" said a voice over the line when a few moments had passed. "This is Lt. Gillespie speaking. Hello?"

Louie tried to get his tongue unstuck from the back of his throat. "It's Louie Hollander, calling about the body," he finally said. "I mean…have you found out who it was or how he…or she…died?"

"She's on ice in the morgue right now," said Lt. Gillespie. "We're still investigating—"

"Sorry, that's all the time you have, " the operator broke in.

Louie hung up the phone and looked over at Charlie. "Well," he said, "at least we found out one thing. The body was the body of a woman."

# CHAPTER 8

# Back Home

Here's cross hand'n ye," Charlie said reluctantly to Louie the next morning when he boarded the train to go back home with Uncle Sam.

After Charlie had left, Louie helped Ma load all the provisions they had collected onto the lighthouse tender that Mr. McAllister had commandeered for their return to Two Tree Island. Included in the provisions were bales of hay, chicken feed, dog food, jugs of drinking water, canned fish, wool, cloth and boxes of other canned food, flour, sugar, salt and coffee.

"Don't forget this pane of glass," said Mr. McAllister, handing Louie the boxed glass. Louie took the glass and found a place on deck where he hoped it wouldn't get broken. He held Scout's collar as the tender's engine turned over and then leaned down to stroke her fur. Scout wagged her tail and licked his face.

"I know. You'll miss them, too."

When the tender came alongside the wharf, Aussie helped them unload the supplies before jumping on board. "Ye'll find everything ship-shape," he said as the tender moved away from the wharf and headed back to the harbor.

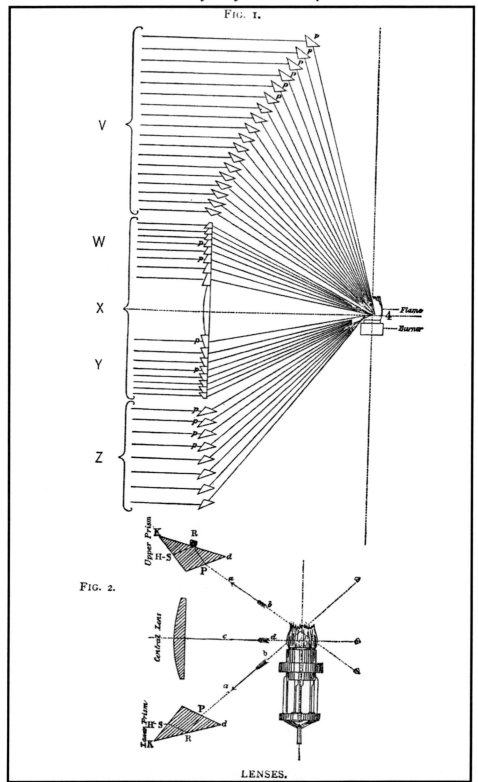

FIG. 1.

FIG. 2.

LENSES.

By the time Louie finished helping Ma put all the supplies where they belonged, the sun had begun its descent into the horizon. Louie walked over to the lighthouse tower to light the lamp. Once there, he walked round and round the Fresnel lens, remembering the geometry assignment Miss Gilbert had given to him. As many times as he had tended this lens he had never thought to figure out how it worked or how it sent its beam of light so far away.

"Ma, can you tell me anything about how our Fresnel lens works?" Louie asked her after supper.

Ma drew a diagram of the lens on a seheet of paper.

"You see these triangles at the points I've marked $p$ for prism? They form a continuous line and make a shape like the outside of half of a round barrel. There are several rings of glass laid on top of one another. The first eight (marked $z$) are fitted into frames of bronze that separate one from another. The next eight (marked $y$) with the broad band (marked $x$) and the eight above (marked $w$) are set close together. Above this middle part ($y$, $z$, $x$ and $w$) are 18 other prisms like the first ones (marked $v$)."

Louie looked closely at the drawing.

"I still don't get it," he said. Scout grunted.

"Look at the lamp lighting this room."

Louie looked up at the kerosene lamp that was burning over their heads.

"That lamp gives off light beams that are reflected back at us," Ma continued. "What Mr. Fresnel, a French inventor, figured out was how to design a lens that would hold those wandering light beams from the lamp so they wouldn't get lost in the darkness of the night by shooting up into the sky in every direction and then down into the ocean to be lost. What he designed was a set of prisms that would bend the light beams."

"Huh?" said Louie, his mouth dropping open.

"He designed the lens with all these prisms to focus the bent light rays into a beam that could shoot out over the water."

"But how do the prisms bend the beams?" Louie was trying to absorb this amazing new knowledge.

"Well, it's a scientific fact that when light passes from a transparent medium—such as air, glass or water—to another, as long as the mediums are of different hardness or density, the beams are bent or turned from their natural course. Now, is glass harder than air?"

Louie nodded.

"Another word for 'hardness' is 'density,'" Ma continued. "The bending of the light beams is called 'refraction.' Because the prisms are at different slopes or angles, they reflect the beams of light into a powerful ray that is then directed out into the ocean. The barrel, or round shape, helps keep the light beam together. The smaller the order of the Fresnel lens, the farther the light beam is projected. The first-order lenses can actually transmit a beam that can be seen for up to 25 miles."

"Because there are more prisms to refract the light!" exclaimed Louie.

"Right! Well, that's enough for now. When we extinguish the flame tomorrow, you can sketch our Fresnel lens so that all the prisms of glass are accounted for."

That night, Louie lay in bed and watched the powerful light beam careen across his window. He counted the seconds between beams—and fell asleep dreaming of prisms of light dancing across the sky. Scout curled up under the quilt at his feet and snored softly.

# CHAPTER 9

# The Wright Flight

Louie watched for Gus's mail boat.
Gus's visits grew fewer and farther between as the winter weather set in. Louie hungered for news of the outside world. *Only the letters and catalogs Gus brings in his boat relieve the monotony of this desolate island,* he thought.

Two weeks after Thanksgiving, the weather cleared enough for Gus to arrive with letters for Louie and Ma. When Louie opened Uncle Sam's letter, several newspaper articles with pictures fell out. Louie read the headline from one of the articles. "Man Flies!" it read. Louie read the first paragraph: "On Monday, December 17, two brothers named Wilbur and Orville Wright made a gasoline-powered aeroplane fly into the air at Kitty Hawk, North Carolina."

Next, Louie opened Charlie's letter. "Can you believe it?" he read. "These two brothers made this thing go up into the air and fly."

Louie looked at the picture Charlie had cut out of the paper, and then continued reading. "A life-saving crew helped these two guys lug this heavy thing—it weighed 600 pounds—up a big hill.

They pushed it down the hill on a monorail, like the slip your dory goes down. At first it didn't work and the thing crashed at the bottom of the hill in the sand.

"But two days later, they tried it again. This time, they laid the track on flat sand. One brother, Orville, was at the controls while the other brother, Wilbur, ran alongside. With the help of a 23-mile per hour wind, the thing actually lifted off the ground for 120 feet. Can you imagine? They tried it three more times. The third time, the aeroplane (as they call it) got 852 feet off the ground and stayed up for almost a minute."

*Gosh*, Louie thought. He looked up at a seagull flying overhead. *Wish I could go up in the air like that.* He went back and read Uncle Sam's letter.

Dear Louie,

A friend from Dayton, Ohio, sent me this clipping and I thought I'd share it with you and your mother. The article came from a Dayton newspaper. Orville and Wilbur Wright are the grown sons of a man I knew at seminary, who is now a bishop. Apparently, one of his sons sent this telegram:

Success—four flights Thursday morning—all against 21 mile wind—started from level with engine power alone—average speed through air 31 miles—longest 57 seconds—inform press— home Christmas—stop.[1]

When I last heard from the bishop, his sons had started a bicycle shop in Dayton and were experimenting with gliders. They would actually fly off hills in these things. Apparently, this time they had a gasoline-powered engine in one of their gliders.

Thinking of you both. Hope to visit after Christmas.

—Uncle Sam

Louie took the newspaper clippings upstairs and thought about Miss Gilbert's assignment. *Should I write about the Wright brothers and their aeroplane or Mr. Marconi's wireless? Did anybody think they were cranks?*

He flipped through the pages of the dictionary on the shelf near his bed to find the meaning of the noun "crank." There were three definitions. He thought the last one might fit people who liked to try new ways of doing things: "An annoyingly eccentric person or one that is overly enthusiastic about a particular subject or activity." Now he had the beginning of his paper. But first he needed to write back to Charlie and Uncle Sam. One never knew when Gus might return in his mail boat—and Christmas was only five days away.

---

[1] Telegram sent by Wilbur and Orville Wright to their father on December 17, 1903.

# Chapter 10

# Preparations

*What can I give Ma for Christmas?*

Louie was at a loss this year. Gift buying was out. He and Charlie hadn't had time to shop, anyway. They'd been too busy sleuthing. Last year, he had carved a bird.

"What do you think?" he asked Scout the next morning. He had just extinguished the lamp and was in the process of drawing a picture of the Fresnel lens.

"Woof!" was Scout's only reply. She wagged her tail.

Suddenly, an idea clicked in Louie's head. *I'll draw a picture of Scout and make a wooden frame!* he thought.

After he had finished drawing the Fresnel lens and Ma had approved it, Louie began drawing his picture of Scout. He worked on it in his loft bedroom when he knew Ma was busy in the kitchen or in between lessons in the lighthouse tower.

The weather turned colder and the seas became choppier. Except for Gus in his mail boat, Two Tree Island didn't have any other visitors for days. Snow flurries greeted Louie when he went out to milk Betsy. As he picked up the milk pail and headed for the house with Scout at his heel, he thought to himself, *Time will move quickly if I keep busy.*

Just as he was about to open the front door, Scout picked up her ears, turned and bolted down the hill. Louie whistled and called her to come, but something else had caught her attention, and she started barking. Louie put the pail down and headed down the hill toward the wharf. When he got to the top of the steps, he looked down. There below, the *Rainbow* was just pulling up alongside the wharf.

A man in the stern, wearing a red coat, was waving to him. *It couldn't be,* thought Louie. But the red-sleeved hand waving had fur trim—and the person waving looked just like…Santa Claus!

"Ho! Ho! Ho!" called the Santa Claus figure. "Sled broke down and had to make me rounds in this here boat. Got a bag of goodies for ye."

Captain Bowline maneuvered the boat up beside the wharf. As Louie raced down the hill and joined Scout on the wharf, Captain Bowline put the bumpers over the side and threw the lines to Louie, who fastened them to cleats. Then the Captain handed up a cut evergreen tree to Louie, who grabbed it by the top. "Missus and I cut down this here tree for yer Christmas," he said.

"And here's yer presents to put under it," the bearded person added. He handed up a large bag to Louie.

As soon as Louie had the tree and the large bag of gifts up on the wharf, Captain Bowline cast off. "Got to make me rounds 'afore sundown," Santa called as the *Rainbow* pulled away from the wharf. Louie thought he picked up a bit of Scottish brogue as the bearded figure in the stern called out, "Merry Christmas!"

*Now it will seem like Christmas is coming,* Louie thought as he climbed up the winding, steep steps with the tree. Ma was waiting at the door of the house to help him bring the tree in and set it in a corner of the room.

"Who brought us this?" she asked Louie. She had been busy in the kitchen baking cookies and hadn't heard or seen the *Rainbow.*

"Capt'n Bowline said he and Mrs. Bowline cut it themselves. And someone who looked just like Santa left a big bag of gifts."

"Well I'll be," Ma replied. "I'll get my shawl and help you carry the bag up the steps."

For the next two days, Louie and Ma decorated their tree. First, Louie built a wooden stand for it. Then they popped corn over the coal stove, strung the popped kernels together with cranberries, and hung the strands around the tree. *Great food for the birds,* Louie thought as he placed the last strand around the bottom of the tree. Ma dug out three special blown-glass ornaments that had been carefully tucked away in the corner of her trunk. She clipped them onto the ends of the branches. Louie carved and painted a seagull and fixed a nest for it to rest on.

"Looks just like Sammy," said Ma, admiring Louie's creation.

*So it does,* thought Louie as he continued carving some small round balls and then painted faces on them. Ma found some scraps of yarn and fabric and made the bodies of little people.

"Look at this one," she said, holding up one of the finished figures. "Who do you guess this is?"

Louie looked up from the face he was painting. The little man had a mustache and wore a double-breasted blue jacket. "Looks like one of us lighthouse keepers. All he needs is a hat."

"Not quite," Ma replied. "Try again."

Louie thought of all the people he knew who had mustaches and wore blue jackets. He even remembered the man on the steamer— the fat man who had burst one of the pearl buttons off his jacket when he walked up the gangplank.

"Not Mr. McAllister!" Louie laughed. He remembered Mr. McAllister pulling on his mustache and scratching his bald head when Ma had applied for the job as the lighthouse keeper. Louie hadn't liked Mr. McAllister back then because he had called him "boy." He still had mixed feelings about the lighthouse superintendent.

Last of all, Louie cut up pages of the Sears and Roebuck catalog and made paper ornaments out of them. When they were finished, he strung them around the tree.

"Oh Tannenbaum, oh Tannenbaum," Ma hummed as she stood back and admired their creation. Louie joined her as they held hands and sang the familiar German carol.

Time went by quickly as they prepared for the big day.

# CHAPTER 11

# A Whiteout Christmas

I t's snowing, Ma!"

Louie looked out of his loft bedroom window. The light coming from the lighthouse beacon illuminated snowflakes of all sizes and shapes as they floated past. Over on the foot of his bed, Louie spied his old stocking.

"Woof! Woof!" barked Scout. She shook herself, sniffed at something in the stocking, and started chewing it.

"Hey, wait a minute," said Louie. He wrestled the stocking out of Scout's teeth and looked inside. "Something for you and some things for me!" He laughed as he pulled out a red ball on top and threw it across the room for Scout to fetch. Then he reached inside and put his hand around something soft. He pulled out some new gloves, then a pair of earmuffs, and finally some dates and nuts.

"Merry Christmas!" Ma called from the bottom of the steps. "It looks like a white one—visibility still clear, but it may get worse. Come on down and see what Santa has brought us."

When Louie came downstairs, he couldn't believe his eyes. There under the Christmas tree were many wrapped packages. *Wonder of wonders*, he thought. With the exception of the picture he had made and framed for Ma, there had been only two gifts under the tree when he had gone to bed on Christmas Eve. Then he remembered the bag Santa had left along with the tree. Ma must have placed those presents there after he went to sleep.

"One present before breakfast," Ma said as she handed Louie a box. Louie shook the box, but it didn't rattle. "What's your guess?" she asked.

"A scarf." It made sense, because Louie had gotten the gloves in his stocking and seen Ma knitting every night. But instead of a scarf, a sweater greeted him.

"Just what I needed, Ma," said Louie, giving her a kiss. His old sweater had been patched several times and was now too short in the sleeves. "Now here's one for you." He handed Ma a square package. Ma opened it carefully.

"Oh, Louie!" she exclaimed. "It's a drawing of Scout! And so like her!" She sat back and gazed at the picture. Then she turned and beamed at Louie. "You never cease to amaze me with your talents."

By this time, the snow had picked up and they couldn't see the lighthouse tower. "Better go start the fog siren while I fix us some breakfast, " Ma said. Louie put on his new sweater, earmuffs, gloves and boots and went outside into the blizzard.

In between tending the lens in the tower and sounding the fog siren, Louie and Ma opened the rest of their gifts. When he opened his gift from Uncle Sam, Louie exclaimed, "A Brownie box camera! Just what I wished for!" He peered through the lens at Ma. "Hold still," he said. "I'll snap you first."

The other presents, including ones from the Bowlines, Mr. McAllister, Miss Gilbert, and even from the crew of the lighthouse cutter *Woodbury,* didn't thrill Louie as much as his new camera.

Louie became so preoccupied with picking out subjects to photograph that Ma had to remind him when his turn came to go out into the gathering storm so he could tend to the wick and fill the reservoir for the Fresnel lens.

# CHAPTER 12

# Monotony

*Same routine every day,* thought Louie.

Christmas day had come and gone, but the blizzard lingered on. It seemed to Louie like time was standing still between tending the lighthouse beacon and keeping the fog siren blaring. He took to putting his earmuffs on while inside so he could muffle the piercing sounds from the foghorn and finish reading *Uncle Tom's Cabin.* When he came to the part about Eliza jumping from ice floe to ice floe to escape capture, he wondered if the ocean surrounding their small island had frozen, too.

*What would it be like to be a slave?* he thought. *To be owned by others…to be taken away from your mother and father…to be sold to another owner?* Louie couldn't imagine being separated from Ma, even though being around her all the time often got on his nerves. Yet at other times, he also felt like a slave—a slave to his duties at the lighthouse tower and to his lessons. *Once in a while, I'd like some free time to do whatever I want when I feel like doing it,* he said to himself.

Ma's constant refrain these days seemed to be, "Louie, it's your turn." She woke him up even while he was in the middle of a dream.

He had to roust himself out of his warm bed, put on his sweater and coat, and brace himself to meet the wintry blasts. Sometimes Louie woke up Scout—who was usually snoring softly at the foot of his bed—and sometimes he let her sleep. Scout was dog-tired, too.

On this particular night, he had just dozed off to sleep after his night turn when he heard Ma's voice. "What?" he mumbled from under the quilt.

"Louie," said Ma, shaking him awake. "I don't feel well. I hurt all over. Can you take my shift?"

The lantern Ma held illuminated her flushed cheeks. Louie put out his hand to touch her forehead. "Ma, you're burning up. Go back to bed. I'll take over."

"Put some snow in a bucket when you return," Ma said. "When it melts, you can help me bring down the fever with the cold water."

As soon as Ma was settled back in her bed, Louie left for the lighthouse tower. When he finished winding the wench and trimming the wick, he wrote in the log:

*Blizzard conditions. No relief in sight. Keeper sick.*
                                                                —Louie Hollander

# CHAPTER 13

# Coping

Snow turned to rain.

The rain made a crust on top of the snow so that shoveling became impossible. It turned to ice when it hit the ground, making the walkway between the tower and the house slippery.

*Need to figure a way to get to the tower and the cow shed so I can milk Betsy,* thought Louie. He looked around for something that would give him some traction on the slippery walk. There, in the corner of the hen house, he spied the dust bucket. He hadn't had time to clean it—he had been too busy just keeping the light beacon from going out—so there was a lot of coal dust still in it.

Louie shoveled some wood ashes from the fireplace into another bucket and spread both on the walkway for traction. When he tried walking on the icy snow, it crunched under his feet so he could make it to the cow shed without slipping. But Scout skidded and tumbled down the slight hill to the shed.

"Come on girl, we can make it back up the hill," he coaxed when he had finished milking Betsy. He grabbed Scout's collar with one hand so she wouldn't slip backward, and grabbed the pail of milk with the other. The crusted snow bristled and crackled under his feet, but they managed to get to the kitchen before all the milk had spilled out of the can.

By now, Louie had added cooking to his lighthouse duties. At least he could open some cans and boil water to make tea and milk for Ma. He fried some eggs the hens had laid and took breakfast up to Ma.

Even though he had brought snow in and melted it to cool down Ma's fever, she didn't seem to get much better. Ma was the one to take care of him when he was sick, but now she was so weak that all she could do was direct Louie in the ways of the kitchen and call to him when it was time to trim the wick or wind up the wench. How he wished for Uncle Sam's presence with them now.

*Got to keep the lamp lit…got to take care of Ma,* Louie repeated several times a day as he dragged himself from the kitchen to the tower to the fog horn and back to Ma. Once he tripped over Scout because he forgot she was there. But he kept on going. He had to.

# CHAPTER 14

# Dark Night

*N*eed to sleep…just for a few minutes…

Louie fell on top of his loft bed—coat and boots still on. Scout woofed and sprawled beside him. The light beacon danced across the room. The fog siren kept up its bleating sound. Then there was no sound except the waves slapping against the shoreline.

*"Louie! Louie!"* Someone, somewhere, was calling for him to come. He strained to go, but he couldn't move his legs. *Got to go,* he said to himself, but his feet were like lead ballast. Now there were more voices. The voices turned into the calls of seagulls—*caw, caw*—all around his head. He tried to swat them away, but his arms wouldn't move. The birds became bats, slapping their wings in his face. *Scout, Scout*—she was way over there, going into the sea. *No, Scout! Come back!* But it was too late. Scout was gone. He tried to scream but no words came out. *Quiet—so quiet. Dark—so dark.*

"Louie, wake up!"

He felt someone shaking him and heard a voice calling him again. Then he felt something wet on his face. He opened his eyes. Scout was licking his cheeks.

The darkness and quiet startled him awake. Louie sat up and rubbed his eyes. He couldn't see anything. Then he knew that the voice was Ma's.

"Ma? Are you better?"

"Yes, it's me. Go over to the tower and find out what's happened to the light. It's gone out. The fog siren's stopped, too. We have to get them fixed. I'll come with you."

"But…but you're sick," Louie protested.

"It can't be helped. We have to get that wick burning again."

"Here," Louie said, "take my hand." He groped around with his other hand until he felt the lantern on the table beside his bed. Ma helped him light it. He held it up high so they could see where they were going as they cautiously walked across to the tower. After they were inside, Ma had to sit down on the winding staircase.

"Go on up without me, Louie," she said. "I'll catch up." Halfway up the stairs, Louie heard her coughing. He stopped climbing and came back down to her side.

"Go on up," she demanded.

When Louie reached the platform at the top of the tower where the Fresnel lens rested, he held the lantern up high to look around. *Eerie,* he thought. Everything was so still and quiet. His ears weren't used to all the silence. He looked over at the lens. Not only had it stopped rotating, but no flame came from the wick.

By the time Louie had wound the mechanism and filled the reservoir, Ma had joined him. Together, they trimmed the wick and tried to light it—but it wouldn't light.

"The wick must have gotten dry," said Ma. "I wonder how long it has been out?" They tried several more times until the wick finally ignited.

Louie took the spyglass and looked out into the night. He followed the beacon of light as it traveled around Two Tree Island. Then he saw something that made his heart stop. It was a ship's mast.

"Oh God…no!" he gasped.

# CHAPTER 15

# Mishap

L ook out! The reef!" Louie screamed.
He waved his arms, hoping the ship out there could see him
or the rocks.

"Ring the bell! Behind the tower!" Ma shouted. "Maybe they'll hear it before…"

Louie was down the tower steps before Ma could finish. He reached the bell and pulled the rope leading to the clapper. But even before the clapper hit the bell casing, he heard the crash.

Ma appeared at his side with the lantern. "Quick, Louie! We have to see what we can do to help."

With Scout at his heels, Louie crunched his way through the snow to the boathouse where their double-ended dory was stored for the winter. The rain had stopped and a full moon illuminated the outline of the four-masted schooner. The ship's stern was nearest shore with her bow out to sea.

Louie could hear men shouting above the surf. Ma came alongside. "Wait," she called. "Let's try to hail them first before we take our boat out in this weather. We'll see if they have a dory on board that they can use to get to shore."

Ma handed Louie the megaphone. Louie moved cautiously over the slippery rocks until he was in hailing distance.

"Ahoy! Anybody!" he cried. He thought he saw movement and heard a splash. *Hope it's their dory hitting the water and not people jumping into the frigid ocean,* he thought. He shivered just thinking about the latter.

Just as he and Ma were about to launch the double ender, he saw a shape moving across the water.

"This way!" Ma took the megaphone from Louie and shouted. "Follow the lantern!" Louie held the lantern and moved it from side to side. They heard the splash of the oars and saw four figures illuminated by the moonlight in the boat.

"Anybody else still on board?" Ma asked as she and Louie hauled the dory up the slip.

"The captain!" one of the voices cried. "He stayed behind and—"

"Save him!" a woman's voice shouted hysterically. "The boat's taking on water real fast."

"Got some life-saving gear here," Louie interrupted. "Help me with the Lyle gun so I can get the buoy out there."

"But we can't see!" the woman's voice wailed. Just then, the sky seemed to lighten a bit. *Was that lightning?* Louie thought he saw a flash.

"Be dawn soon," said a calmer voice. "We can see to launch her better then. Used to be on a life-saving station up north—let's git 'er ready. No time for wimperin'—all hands needed." The man who had spoken jumped out of the dory as Louie hauled the boat up the slip.

"Git the rope in that thar box," the man commanded another person in the boat. "Don't need no hysterical women folk. If ye want to save 'em, give a hand. Careful…" The man assisted the woman out onto the shore.

Louie helped the seamen move the box and get the Lyle gun up the shore closer to where the ship was foundering on the reef. Ma began coughing again.

"Please, Ma, go back to the house where it's warm," said Louie. "You, too, ma'am," he added to the wailing woman behind him.

Dawn climbed up over the horizon. *Hurrah,* thought Louie. *Now we can see to fire the gun.* Then he prayed, "God, please keep the ship from sinking before we get this set up." Waves broke over the bow as the ship listed to one side. Louie could see two figures clinging to the aft mast.

"All set. Ready…fire!" The gun shot the rope toward the men on the ship's stern, but it fell short and landed in the water.

"Douglas!" the seaman who had assumed command said to another seaman. "Go see if you can git that dory back out to 'em while we re-fire this darn thing."

"I'll go, too," Louie offered.

Louie helped push the dory back into the water while Douglas manned the oars. When the dory hit the first wave, frigid water came over the boat and slapped Louie in the face. The dory made it over the first wave and then the second. As they neared the foundering ship, Louie heard the "pop, bang" of the Lyle gun as the seamen on shore shot off the rope again. This time, the tally landed on the ship's stern. As they drew nearer, Louie could see that the rope was now fastened to the mast. The seamen on land were paying out the buoy over the rope toward the ship.

"Stand clear," Douglas warned. "Don't want to be sucked into a whirlpool if'n she starts to go down."

Louie could see someone climbing into the breeches buoy. He watched from the stern seat of the dory as it bobbed up and down with the swells. The buoy slowly made its way back to the island and to safety.

"How many left on board?" Louie asked Douglas.

"The captain and the cook, methinks," answered the seaman. Louie watched as the buoy made its way back to the foundering ship. He heard a horrible groan and crackling as the ship's bow began to sink into the sea.

"Oh no!" Louie screamed. The buoy made it back to the stern and another person climbed into it. Louie knew that the captain would be the last to be rescued. *But what would happen to him when the ship sank?*

"If you can get closer, maybe he can jump," he said to Douglas.

"Want us to crack up on them thar rocks, too?"

Louie could see the captain standing in front of the mast, which was now tilting at a dangerous 45-degree angle toward the sea. He watched as the captain untied the rope from the mast and then, still holding on to the rope, jumped away from the sinking stern into the broiling sea. Douglas deftly headed the dory toward the figure bobbing in the water.

"Grab that rope with the boat hook," he shouted at Louie. Louie reached over with the hook and pulled on the rope when the dory reached it. He hauled in the wet rope until the captain came alongside and then dragged him over the side and into the dory. Louie took off the captain's coat and covered him with his own. The man's beard was now covered with icicles and his face was turning a grayish-white.

"Hurry and get us back before hypothermia sets in," cried Louie. He threw his own body over the captain to help put some warmth back into the man's cold body. He covered the captain's mouth with his, willing him to live.

The seamen on land met the dory and hauled her up the slip. Louie felt the captain's chest moving under his own. Louie's own shivering body alerted the seamen.

"Come on now, lad. Let's git both of ye to some warmth."

# CHAPTER 16

# Making Do

"…c…c…can't…g…g…get warm."

Louie couldn't make his teeth stop chattering, even though he had his feet in a bucket of warm water and a blanket wrapped around him. Scout jumped up and licked his face.

"Y…y…y…your…t…t…tongue feels warm." Louie wrapped his arms around Scout. The blanket fell to the ground. One of the seamen named Harry picked it up and put it back around his shoulders.

Louie by now had met all of the persons rescued from the *Sea Mist*. He learned that was the name of the schooner that had sunk off the island. He had helped some of the men shed their wet clothes and lent them blankets or some of his dry clothes. Many of the men had on their oilskins, so they were dry underneath.

The seamen removed Captain Jack's wet and almost frozen clothes and covered him with warm towels. As he sat there shivering, Louie heard the men calling the woman, Evelyn. She caressed the captain's cheeks and started to rub his hands and feet to restore the circulation but stopped when his skin started to flake off in her hands. She screamed. Ma came over to calm her down and bandage the captain's hands.

Besides Douglas and Harry, the other men were Albert and Abram. Louie thought Abram looked to be about his age. They called the cook Bohai. Louie guessed they called him that because he looked Chinese.

Ma hung the wet clothes all around their pot-bellied stove and in front of the fireplace. "Got to Capt'n Jack just in time—afore the 'thermia did him in," said Douglas. "Thanks to this lad here, we saved 'im." Douglas nodded and grinned at Louie, but Louie wasn't sure he deserved the praise, after letting the lamp go out.

"Are any of you men dry enough to get some more coal for the stove?" said Ma.

"I'll go," Abram said. "Just tell me where."

"In the coal shed, down those steps. Don't fall—it might be slippery. Better spread some ashes first."

"Here, I'll join ye," said Harry. He looked over at Ma, who was busy heating up some oatmeal on the stove in between coughing spells. "Anything else we can do, ma'am?" he said. "Sounds like you ain't too well."

"The lamp needs to be extinguished."

"But Ma," Louie complained. "They don't know how."

"Be still now and git warm," said Harry. "I've tended a lamp or two."

"It can wait until you've all had something warm in your stomachs," said Ma. "Just sit for a while. It won't hurt the lamp to burn a bit longer." Eventually, it was only Abram and Harry who had to leave the warmth of the small kitchen.

Louie looked around at their unexpected guests, who sat crowded around their small table. "I'm sorry about your ship," he said. "I'm glad you all made it to shore."

"I was at the wheel when we saw the beam from your lighthouse tower come round," said Albert. "I turned her hard to starboard when I realized Capt'n was a-callin', but her stern struck 'afore we could clear the reef."

*If only*…thought Louie and hung his head. Now all they could do would be to carry on and share their meager provisions until the weather cleared up enough for help to arrive.

# CHAPTER 17

# Sharing and Caring

O atmeal nevah tasted so good!"

Captain Jack's words warmed Louie's heart. Evelyn was spooning the oatmeal into his mouth. His hands were still wrapped and his feet had begun to swell, but Louie hoped he wouldn't have to have them cut off like Ben. Louie had stopped shivering.

After all the blankets, quilts and extra dry clothes had been distributed, and Harry and Abram had returned with the coal, Harry extinguished the lamp wick.

"We were headed for Rockland with our cargo when she hit," said Captain Jack between mouthfuls of oatmeal.

"What cargo?" asked Louie.

"Sardines, mostly. Hoped to get Abram here, my boy, home in time for school after his Christmas break."

"And get paid for our catch," Evelyn added. "Papa will be really mad."

"We're still celebrating Christmas here," said Louie, trying to refocus the conversation to Christmas. He gestured toward the decorated tree in the corner of the parlor. Most of its needles had fallen off, and Ma and Louie's opened presents lay scattered about. Since Ma had been sick, they had not had time to put any of their gifts away. Louie pointed to the sweater Abram was now wearing.

"That's the sweater Ma made and gave me for Christmas," he continued.

"Sun's out," said Harry. "Storm seems to have let up. Let's go see if Davy Jones's Locker has spared us some supplies. Heave to, me lads."

Albert, Harry and Douglas donned their dried out oilskins and boots.

"Anyone here know how to milk a cow?" Louie asked.

The three seamen shook their heads.

"Bohai can do," said a voice. The Chinese cook's pigtail bobbed. He crossed his arms and bowed toward Louie.

Louie gave Bohai the milk pail. The cook followed the others out the door backward, still bowing to Louie. Suddenly, Scout leapt up and rushed through his legs, sending him sprawling.

"Just hold on to the milk can on your way back," said Louie. He could barely get the words out because he was laughing so hard. "And watch that Scout doesn't knock it over, too."

Louie looked over at Abram, who was edging over toward the opened presents under the tree. "Here, you can look through my new kaleidoscope," Louie said, picking it up and handing it to him. Louie hadn't had a chance to even look through it himself.

Captain Jack went back to sleep. Louie thought Evelyn might help Ma, but instead she said, "I need some fresh clothes—this dress needs washing."

"Okay, but can you wait a moment?" said Ma. "I need to take stock of…" But Ma couldn't finish her sentence before a coughing fit seized her again.

When Bohai returned with the milk pail, he examined all the food supplies in the kitchen. "Bohai make do. Take care of Ma," he said as he put a teapot on the stove to boil.

Harry and Douglas returned with a barrel full of sardines. Albert carried a trunk. "Couple of other barrels still down there," said Harry as he put the barrel outside the front door.

*Just like the quail in the wilderness, God has provided,* Louie said to himself. "I hope you know lots of recipes for sardines," he said to Bohai.

"Bohai can make." He said as his pigtail bobbed up and down.

# CHAPTER 18

# Getting Acquainted

They were now packed in like sardines.

Louie had once visited a sardine plant with his pa and watched as the workmen on the assembly lines stuffed as many sardines into each passing can as they could.

After each person had said, "I'm thawing out" or "I'm warming up," they had decided on their sleeping places. Ma insisted that Captain Jack and Evelyn have her bedroom while she lay down on the settee in the parlor. Now, crammed into a single bed with Abram, Louie felt like a sardine. He slept fitfully, listening to Ma's coughing and Bohai, sleeping on the cot beside him in the loft, grinding his teeth. Each time Abram turned over in his bed, Louie ended up on the floor. Finally, Louie wrapped up in his quilt and stayed on the floor with Scout.

During his waking moments, Louie replayed the trauma of the last 24 hours in his head. *If only* Ma hadn't gotten sick; *if only* he had stayed awake to keep the lamp burning; *if only* the ship had been able to turn fast enough not to hit the reef. Shackles of guilt weighed on him. *If only* Uncle Sam were here. He counted the number of times the beacon lit up the room until it was gone.

Finally, toward dawn, he fell asleep, only to be awakened by Albert. Albert, Harry, and Douglas had been assigned to take over tending the lens in the lighthouse tower, after Louie had showed them how everything worked.

"Sorry to wake you up lad, but where do ye keep the kerosene to fill the reservoir?" Albert asked.

Louie got up and, after putting on his coat and boots, showed Albert where the kerosene was kept in the oil house. He helped Albert fill the reservoir, milked Betsy and fed the chickens, gathering the few eggs they had laid during the night.

*Not enough to feed all these people,* Louie thought. *I hope we don't have to kill these chickens to feed the crew.*

As if she could read his thoughts, Ma asked, "Louie, please bring me something to write on. I want to finish taking stock of what we have in the way of provisions."

Louie brought her some paper and a pen. She made her way to the pantry where all the food was shelved and stored. She looked into the barrels and counted the tins. Bohai joined her in the kitchen, and Ma handed him her list.

"Better ration these. It's all we have left." She fell back on her makeshift bed. "My chest feels so heavy."

"Bohai know…take care." He felt Ma's head and put his ear to her chest. Then he turned to Louie and said, "Need camphor."

Louie brought the medicine chest. Bohai took out the camphor bottle and rubbed the liquid on to Ma's chest and back. Louie held his breath as long as he could so he wouldn't breathe in the strong vapor.

"Ah," said Ma, falling back down.

Louie mumbled a prayer, "Please God, do something to make her well." At that moment, he remembered that he had forgotten to raise the SOS flag, so he raised it on their flagpole. Even though the seas were still choppy and it had started to snow again, he continued to pray that some passing ship would see it—maybe Gus in the mail boat or Captain Shiver. We wanted someone to find Doc Bowen and ask him to come to examine Ma.

Meanwhile, Albert and Douglas searched the shoreline for debris from their fishing schooner. They were able to retrieve some barrels, wood from the spars, and some sail canvas and ropes. One of the trunks they rescued contained Evelyn's fancy dresses and jewels. Most of the dresses were waterlogged, so the men hung them out on a new rope line. The dresses became stiff in the cold air.

When Louie finished his lighthouse chores, he found Abram curled up in his loft bed reading the *Adventures of Huckleberry Finn*. "Good story," Louie said as he sat down beside him. "My friend Charlie especially likes that book."

"We're putting on a play at school, and we have to read this story," said Abram. "I play one of the lead characters. I took the book with me to read when Papa asked me to go with them during Christmas break. He doesn't often take me along—he used to take Mama. That is, until…" His voice trailed off.

"I thought Evelyn was your ma," said Louie, giving Abram a puzzled look.

"Nope. My mama's…" Abram's eyes welled up with tears. "She's dead." Abram stopped and ran his sleeve across his wet eyes. "Last time I saw her, she sailed out of the harbor with Papa. Papa said their ship ran into some rough seas. A big rogue wave washed over the deck and took Mama with it. We had her funeral right after Papa's ship returned. I really miss her."

"Guess you and I have something in common," Louie said, putting his arm around Abram. "I lost my pa in a storm. He slipped and fell down the lighthouse tower steps."

Louie paused for a moment and then said, "So, who's the woman with your pa?"

"Oh, *her*," Abram said with a sneer. "Guess she's his new girlfriend. Don't like her much. But after the accident, Papa didn't want to go back out on that ship, so he signed up to captain the *Sea Mist*.

Evelyn's the daughter of the owner. Papa started to fancy her after he became captain, but she's too fancy for me!"

With that, Louie decided it was time to change the subject. "What character are you playing in *Huck Finn*?" he asked.

"I'm ole Jim. Remember him?"

Louie and Abram spent the rest of that morning comparing favorite books and playing Halma and other games Louie had been given for Christmas.

# CHAPTER 19

# Waiting and Watching

Ugh," said Abram.

The cook had just handed him sardine paste on hard tack.

Bohai kept coming up with new ways to fix sardines, but Louie was sick of eating them. All the canned food was now gone—except for the tins of hard tack Douglas had found washed up on shore. They had even slaughtered two of the chickens. Betsy was getting thinner, and Louie was scared that one of the seamen would suggest slaughtering her, too. Louie and Abram scoured the shoreline and gathered some mussels and snails when the tide was low. They tried catching fish off the wharf, but the fish weren't biting.

Ma coughed every time she tried to get up. Once she coughed up bloody phlegm. Captain Jack's hands were healing, but one of his feet still looked swollen and he had green streaks up that leg. Evelyn kept whining and complaining—first about the loss of their ship and then about the food. Harry tried to calm her down whenever she became hysterical. "Now ma'am," he would say, "we're all doin' the best we can."

Captain Jack had recovered enough to have the other crew carry him into the parlor to join them for meals. He asked for some paper to record all the cargo and equipment in their ship. Louie learned that the Northeast Sardine Company, which was run by Evelyn's father, owned the *Sea Mist*. Evelyn told Louie that she hadn't liked living on her papa's old ship. "It's slimy and it smells," was one of her complaints.

*How does he put up with her?* Louie thought to himself. She was such a contrast to his ma, who was capable of doing anything—except now when she was sick. Louie had never met a woman like Evelyn. He couldn't imagine what Captain Jack saw in her. From what he knew about Abram's ma, Evelyn wasn't the least bit like her.

*Harry sure told her off,* thought Louie. He liked Harry, who by now had grown a bushy beard. In fact, he liked having all of them around, especially Abram, because he was about his age and they shared the same love of reading and writing.

Now that Harry, Douglas and Albert were helping with the lighthouse beacon and the fog siren, Louie could spend more time with Abram up in his loft bedroom, reading. They took turns reading to Ma from the Bible. One time, Abram read the story about Paul's shipwreck on the Adriatic Sea, in which 275 people made it safely to the island of Malta. Ma suggested that Louie and Abram each write a story about the shipwreck of the *Sea Mist* and compare it to the biblical story in Acts.

When Abram read the part in the story about the apostle Paul healing the sick on the island, Louie put out a hand to touch Ma's arm and prayed silently that she, too, would be healed.

# CHAPTER 20

# Stories and Songs

"Did ye hear the one about…?"

The nine of them spent their evenings together around the blazing fire in the hearth and sang sea ballads and rounds and told stories. Ma tried singing, but when she started coughing she had to stop.

"Did ye hear the one 'bout the soldier who went a-courtin' his lassie?" Douglas said.

"No, tell it," they all said in unison.

"Here she goes, and where she stops nobody knows:

*Around the corner and under a tree,*
*A sergeant major once said to me,*
*Oh will you marry me?*
*For I would like to know*
*For every time I look in your eyes*
*I always want to go*
*Around the corner and under a tree…"*

And so it went, round and round until their voices were hoarse.

"Did ye hear the story 'bout the mysterious disappearance of the lighthouse keeper's wife?" Albert said.

"No!" the rest said in unison. "Tell us!"

"As the story goes, there was this lighthouse keeper and his wife living out at Martin's Rock. Now, the wife, she wanted her grand pianee on the island, so the lighthouse tender brought it over from the mainland—had a hard time hosting it up the ramp. But the crew got it up there, and she was happy as a clam playin' tunes on her pianee. Her husband just kept lighting the lamp year after year.

"One year, the inspector came round. After checking the lens, the inspector looked all over the island but couldn't find the wife nowhere. Lighthouse keeper said she'd gone to the mainland. Inspector didn't think any more 'bout it 'till he went to leave and saw the lighthouse dory still in the boathouse.

"The inspector went back to the house, 'cause he thought he heard some music—he thought maybe she was a-playin' the pianee. So he went back up to the house, but the pianee wasn't there. The lighthouse keeper said she'd be back tomorrow. The inspector decided to stop back after his rounds the next day, but still she wasn't there. *Strange*, the inspector thought. So he asked the keeper again. Keeper said, 'She's probably delayed.'"

Louie remembered the woman's body he had found washed up on shore. *Could it be her? But no, this was only a story.*

"Nevah did find that lighthouse keeper's wife," continued Albert. "When the old keeper died, the Lighthouse Board couldn't get any new keepers to stay and tend the light. Each new recruit swore the lighthouse was haunted by the ghost of a woman."

"I heard a similar tale about the ghost at the Seguin Light," Abram said. "The lighthouse keeper went mad and smashed the piano with an ax and then used the ax to kill his wife and himself— only as the story goes, it's the tune she used to play that haunts the island."[1]

"I found a dead woman's body washed up on shore," Louie announced to the gathered group. "We investigated but weren't able to find out who she was or what happened to her."

The firelight flickered. Silence reigned. Louie looked around the room at their uninvited guests. Ma was now asleep. Evelyn had a bored look. Captain Jack, who had been brought into the parlor for the storytelling hour, fidgeted in his chair. "Leg hurts…need to lie down," he said.

Douglas and Albert carried him back to Ma's bedroom.

---

[1] See Geoffrey Wolff, *The Edge of Maine* (Washington, D.C.: National Geographic, 2005), p. 77. See also Stephen King, *The Shining* (New York: Pocket Books, 2001).

# CHAPTER 21

# Help Arrives

S hip approaching!" Albert yelled from the catwalk around the lighthouse tower.

Louie and Abram were gathering mussels and snails on the low-lying rocks on the other side of the island when they heard him call. They crunched through the lingering snow up the hill and ran past the keeper's house and down to the wharf to await the arrival of the ship. As the boat drew closer, Louie recognized Gus, the mailman.

"Oh, Gus," he gasped as Gus handed him a packet of letters. "I knew you'd come with the mail. Please…go find Mr. McAllister. We've got a crew of shipwrecked seamen here. The captain's got gangrene and Ma's awful sick. Please…bring Doc and Nurse Figgins…hurry!"

"Will do!" Gus called back. He revved up the engine, and the mail boat shot away from the wharf, sending up spray as she did so.

"And bring us food and supplies!" Louie called, cupping his hands around his mouth so Gus would hear him. "We're starving!"

When the mail boat faded from sight, Louie turned to Abram and said, "Come on…let's tell the others."

"Woof!" echoed Scout as she jumped up to catch a snowball that Abram had thrown in the air. It came down and splattered on her nose. Scout shook her head and wiggled her whole body. Then she came back to Abram and wagged her tail.

"Okay, girl—want another?" Abram made another snowball and this time threw it up the hill. "Now, go fetch!" Scout bounded up the hill. When she got there, she looked around, but the snowball had disappeared.

"Come on, Scout," Louie said as he opened the door. "We'll find a real ball."

Louie gave Ma a bundle of letters. "Gus has gone to get help," he said. "They'll be back soon."

"Thank goodness," said Ma.

Louie and Abram went up to the lighthouse tower to watch through the spyglass for ships. They returned to have their lunch of hard tack and sardines. "The last of 'em," Bohai said. He then passed a plate around with a biscuit for each person.

Louie drank the weak tea that Bohai had fixed to go with his biscuit. He savored each bite of the biscuit, but his stomach still growled. Then he remembered the few snails he had pocketed before Gus had arrived.

"Let's smash these snails to use for bait and see if any fish are biting," he said to Abram as he went out the door. Sunlight peeked through the lingering clouds. The wind had finally died down. Louie and Abram reached the wharf and sat with their poles dangling over the side. As they watched for any sight of a ship in the distance, they hoped that some fish would take the bait.

Just when they had given up all hope of catching a fish and were feeling the cold seeping through their clothes, they saw two shapes coming across Windlass Bay toward the island.

"Do you think those ships could be coming here?" said Abram. When the shapes drew closer, Louie could see that one of them looked like the *Rainbow* and the other like the lighthouse tender. With the tide in and the sea relatively calm, Louie thought the *Rainbow* would be able to safely land alongside the wharf.

"Go up to the house and get one of the crew to row the dory out to the tender when she rounds to the landing site," said Louie to Abram. "I'll help with the *Rainbow*."

Doc Bowen was the first ashore from the *Rainbow*, followed by Nurse Figgins. On the way up to the house from the wharf, Louie told Doc Bowen about Ma's coughing and Captain Jack's bad hands and foot.

"How long was he in that cold water?" Doc Bowen asked.

"Don't think it was more than a few minutes," Louie answered. "We pulled him on board the dory right after he jumped and I laid on top of him to get him warm."

Doc Bowen turned and smiled at Louie. "Smart thinking," he said. "You probably saved his life."

Doc hung his coat on a hook inside the door and went first to check on Ma. He took out his stethoscope and listened to her lungs. "Don't like the sounds in your lungs," he murmured. "Best get you to shore and to the hospital. "

As Doc Bowen examined Ma, Nurse Figgins checked Captain Jack's hands and foot and leg. "This one needs attention, too," she called over to Doc Bowen.

"Best get them both ashore to a hospital."

"How?" asked Abram after two of the crew had gone to the landing site to meet the dory coming back from the tender.

"We can use some of 'em old sails to make a stretcher," said Harry. "Com'on, ye salts, let's git to work." The other seamen joined him. Using some of the spars from the sunken ship they had now piled beside the house to use for firewood, they made a rough stretcher. While they were at work, Mr. McAllister and some sea-men carrying boxes arrived from the landing site.

"What's happened here?" he said when he entered the house. "Who are all these…?" His mouth opened and closed as he raised his hand and pointed around the room.

"About time you got here! We're starving!" Evelyn whined. "What'd you bring in the way of food?"

*And take her back with you,* Louie thought. If he heard another complaint out of that woman, he would have a hard time not stuff-ing her mouth with rags. He went over to help Captain Bowline and Harry lift Ma onto the stretcher, and then threw a quilt over her.

"Can I come with Ma?" he asked.

"Need you here to help tend the lamp," Ma mumbled between coughs.

"Don't worry, lad, I'll stay and help ye," Harry offered.

"I'll see to it that your mother gets the best care," said Mr. McAl-lister. Louie watched helplessly as he tucked the quilt around Ma. "Couldn't tell what you needed in the way of food, so we told Jake just to pack up whatever he thought best." He nodded to the sea-men to stack the boxes in the kitchen. "Didn't know 'bout all these folks, though. Don't see any ship around. You folks visiting?"

"No, our ship sank," said Harry. "Got caught in that reef out there. The capt'n—he's in bad shape, too."

Just then, Doc Bowen came out of the bedroom with his bag.

"Soon as you take Mrs. Hollander, come back for the captain and his missus," Captain Bowline said.

Abram clenched his fists. "That's not—" he started to say, but Louie stopped him.

"Can Abram stay here and help me and Harry tend the light?"

"No," Captain Jack said as he was being lifted onto the stretcher. "Need to get Abram back to school."

Louie's heart was heavy as he watched them all leave. He had enjoyed having them around—all except Evelyn.

Harry put an arm around Louie. "Mr. McAllister promised to bring Aussie with him when he returns," he said.

# CHAPTER 22

# Aftermath

A bed all to himself!

The first night after Abram departed, Louie slept in his bed spread eagle with Scout curled up between his legs. With Harry to help maintain the beacon, he only had to wake up once during the night to tend the lamp. When he woke in the morning, the smell of coffee wafted up the loft steps and tickled his nose. Scout thumped his tail on the bed and burrowed under his arm.

"Hey, stop tickling me," Louie laughed as he stretched and rubbed the sleep out of his eyes. He pulled on his overalls and joined Harry in the kitchen.

"Got lots of cleanin' up to do today," Harry announced after breakfast.

Louie looked around at the boxes still half open and the mess the crew and Evelyn had left. Harry gave Louie the special silk rag used to clean the Fresnel lens and another to clean the inside of the tower windows.

"First the lighthouse lens and windows, and then join me back here. I'll tackle the mess inside the house, and scrub her down with lye soap."

They both worked all morning and into the afternoon, stopping only when the lighthouse tender arrived with the rest of their provisions, straw for Betsy and feed for the one chicken left.

"How's Ma?" Louie asked Mr. McAllister.

"They've given her some medicine and she seems a mite better," said Mr. McAllister. "Said to tell you to get back to your school work."

*She must be feeling better*, thought Louie. *She only reminded me once when she was sick to write a story.* Maybe he would finish writing one now and bring it to her to read.

Mr. McAllister broke in on his thoughts. "Captain Jack tells me his ship wrecked because there wasn't any light beacon coming across the water to warn about the rocks. Lighthouse keeper not doing his job?"

Louie looked down at the floor. Each of Mr. McAllister's words bore the guilt in deeper.

"Yes…I mean no, sir."

"But he's been a brave lad—he rescued us all," said Harry, coming to his defense.

"Still, the missus told her father, who's the ship's owner," said Mr. McAllister. "He's angry at the Lighthouse Board and threatening to sue for their losses. There'll be a hearing. Louie and his mother will need to appear. I understand it happened on your watch." He glared at Louie.

"But Ma was sick…" Louie blurted out.

"Save your defense for the hearing," replied Mr. McAllister.

"I'll be there for ye, laddie," said Aussie, who had just come through the door carrying a load of boxes.

"No, you can't," corrected Mr. McAllister. "You'll need to be here, tending the light. He turned back to Louie. "We'll come to fetch you when the hearing is scheduled."

"When can I see Ma?" Louie wished she were here now.

"If the weather holds, I'll ask Captain Bowline to come fetch ye. Now mind these two." Mr. McAllister donned his cap and jacket to go back to the tender. "Oh, almost forgot." He reached in his pocket and drew out a packet of envelopes tied with a string. "Gus told me to give ye these."

# CHAPTER 23

# Suspicious Identity

D on't mind him," Aussie said. He gave Louie a bear hug. "That man's bark is wors'n his bite. Now disappear with them letters whilst Harry and I find places for all this stuff. Git now. Scout, you too." Aussie scratched Scout behind her ears and then shooed her up the loft stairs after Louie.

Louie tore open the first letter. He could tell immediately by the writing that it was from Charlie.

Dear Louie,

How have you been? Any of the blizzards we've had of late hit Two Tree Island? We've had our share of school closings, so we got to enjoy some sledding. Even got to wear Ben's big snow boots.

Speaking of Ben, he's healing okay on his hands—feeling has come back on his two fingers, and he's learning to write with them. He gets around with a cane and has been trying out a prosthesis leg, or peg leg, I call it. He's been doing lots of reading about the Marconi Wireless. Says he wants to be an operator of one of them on a ship. Don't know how he's going to do it with just those two fingers, but once Ben makes up his mind to do something he usually does it.

I've been continuing my investigating to find out more about that woman's body you found. Sheriff says he thinks she may be Captain Spade's wife from Rockland. Had a funeral for her, but no body. She's the only one of the persons reported lost at sea around here.

*Captain Spade,* thought Louie. *Suppose that's Captain Jack? Never did get his last name.* Louie continued reading the letter:

They're trying to reach the captain, but he took off for a fishing trip and hasn't arrived back yet. I'll keep you posted.

Here's cross hand'n ye.

—Charlie

"Course they couldn't reach him," Louie said out loud. "He was here with us." Scout barked and wagged her tail.

"Harry!" Louie called down the stairs.

"What's up lad?" Aussie answered. "He's over 'ta check out the lamp."

Louie grabbed his jacket and gloves, leapt down the stairs and ran past Aussie out the door. He crunched through the snow to the lighthouse tower and climbed the winding staircase steps two by two. When he reached the platform at the top, he found Harry trimming the wick and pouring kerosene into the reservoir.

"Harry…" Louie stopped to catch his breath. "What's Captain Jack's last name?"

"Spade," said Harry.

"I knew it!" Louie exclaimed. "I bet that's his wife's body that washed up on our island."

"Hmm. Heard Abram talking about his mama bein' washed overboard. How'd they know it was her?"

"Don't know—they couldn't find Captain Spade to identify the body. Wonder if he's still in the hospital where Ma is?"

Louie went back to the house and opened the second letter. Some other papers fell out with her note. The letter was from Miss Gilbert.

Dear Louie,

How are you doing with your assignments? Are you keeping up with your geometry lessons? What about those papers I asked you to write? Have you finished reading *Uncle Tom's Cabin?* I'm enclosing those examinations I told you I would send after Christmas. Have your mother monitor you and then have her return them to me, along with your book report and the papers I asked you to write.

—Miss Gilbert

Louie took the letter and examination papers downstairs and threw them on the table. He plopped down on the chair, put his chin on his hands and groaned. "How am I going to take these examinations with Ma in the hospital? I haven't even had time to keep up with the lessons I'm supposed to have completed."

"Well, laddie, git to a-studyin' then. Won't do ye no good to sit here a-moanin'." Aussie turned back to opening boxes and stowing the cans and packages on the kitchen shelves.

# CHAPTER 24

# Writing Assignments

**W**hich writing project comes first? thought Louie.
*Should I write the comparison story of the two shipwrecks,
the book report on* Uncle Tom's Cabin, *or the essay pre-
dicting an invention that would be successful?*

This dilemma haunted Louie for days. He would sit on his bed
with pad of paper and pencil in hand, write a few words and then
scratch them out, crumple up the paper and throw it in the corner.
Scout ran to retrieve each crumpled-up ball. Louie taught her to
drop it into a pail after retrieving it. The pail was almost full when
Louie finally decided he would write the book report on *Uncle
Tom's Cabin.* Of course, he couldn't write the book report until he
had finished reading the last two chapters, so he curled up on his
bed to read.

When he finished reading, he plopped the book down beside
his bed and pondered the question posed by Miss Gilbert. *What
have I learned about slavery?* he thought. *Well, first of all, Harriet
Beecher Stowe described two types of slave owners: the kind ones and
the mean ones.* Louie picked up his pad of paper and pencil and
made a note about that thought. *Then the author created two kinds*

*of slaves: Uncle Tom, the older slave, who submitted to being a slave and survived because of his Christian faith; and George, who craved freedom and escaped.*

He wondered why Mrs. Stowe shared the fate of two Georges at the end of the book: George, the former slave who decided he couldn't claim to be an American and moved to Africa to found the free country of Liberia; and George, the son of a kind white slave owner who purchased freedom for all the slaves on his father's plantation. *Slavery leaves scars,* he thought.

*Now what does slavery have to do with the Civil War?* He had just decided to ask Harry and Aussie that question at supper when he heard Aussie calling, "Mail boat approaching!"

Louie grabbed his coat and pulled on his boots. He yelled for Scout to follow him and ran out the door. He reached the top of the hill just as Gus neared the wharf. "Got a message to pick you up on my route and take ye to the mainland to visit yer Ma," yelled Gus. "How fast can ye git ready? Got a few deliveries to make and then I'll be back." Gus turned his boat around and shot out of sight.

Aussie came up behind Louie. "Best git packin'," he said. "Harry and I will just have to git 'long without ye."

Back at the house, Louie threw some clothes into his duffel along with his writing pad and pencil. *Maybe Ma will help me with my book report,* he thought. He was ready and waiting when Gus returned from his mail rounds. With fair weather and a following wind, the small vessel crossed the bay in record time.

When they neared the landing, Louie thought he saw a familiar figure waiting on the town wharf. *Could it be?*

"Uncle Sam!" Louie exclaimed. "Boy, am I ever glad to see you!"

Uncle Sam's somber face quickened Louie's heart. "How's Ma? Have you seen her? Is she okay?" The questions spilled over each other in their rush to get out.

Uncle Sam hugged Louie, and then stood back and took a long breath before answering. "She's pretty sick, Louie. She has pneumonia. The doctors had to do a gram stain to make sure it wasn't the contagious kind. The hospital put her in isolation when she first arrived. As soon as they said she could have visitors, Captain Bowline called me and then asked Gus to fetch you from Two Tree Island."

Louie and Uncle Sam climbed into the buggy waiting for them. "She will get well, won't she?" asked Louie.

"I certainly hope so, Louie."

# CHAPTER 25

# Hospital Vigil

A woman in gray met Louie and Uncle Sam at the door. "You must be Mrs. Hollander's son," she said to Louie. "She's so proud of you." The woman led the way down a narrow corridor.

"She's really a Sister of Charity," Uncle Sam whispered to Louie, "but all the sisters dress in gray, so they're called 'Gray Ladies.' They run this hospital."

The Gray Lady stopped outside a closed door and handed each of them a mask with which to cover their noses and mouths. "She's in this room," she said. "You must wear these masks and not stay more than half an hour. If she starts to cough, you should leave. There's a room down at the end of this hallway where you can sit. The cafeteria is in the basement if you want some coffee or something to eat."

The Gray Lady opened the door and said, "Mrs. Hollander, you have some visitors."

Louie choked the tears back when he looked at Ma lying on the bed. She had a tent around her head and an oxygen-pumping machine beside her that made a whizzing noise.

"I missed you, Louie," said Ma. "I'm glad you both came." Louie could see her chest rise and fall as she labored to breathe and talk at the same time. "Who's tending the lamp?"

"Aussie's come to help," replied Louie. "I've been working on my school work, Ma."

She nodded and then turned to speak to Uncle Sam. "Will you pray for me?"

Uncle Sam knelt down beside the bed and took Ma's hand in his. Louie came over and knelt beside him and held her other hand. They prayed that Ma would get well. *Please God, heal Ma,* Louie prayed silently. *I can't lose both her and Pa.* Louie had never wanted anything so desperately.

"Thank you…" Ma said, but then started to cough. Uncle Sam motioned to Louie, and the two of them left the room. When they reached the sitting room at the end of the hall, Louie buried his head against Uncle Sam's chest and sobbed.

"It's…my…fault…" he cried.

"Why?" Uncle Sam asked.

"'Cause I let the lamp go out. 'Cause she went outside in the cold to help. 'Cause…"

Uncle Sam stopped him. "Let's sit down, and then you can tell me the whole story." He led Louie over to two chairs in the corner of the sitting room. Eventually, Louie stopped crying long enough to tell Uncle Sam about the shipwreck and the upcoming hearing.

"You couldn't help it that your mother got sick, Louie. Being tired is not a sin."

"But letting the light beacon go out is. Ma might lose her job."

"We'll see about that. You're both very special to God."

The two sat and talked until it was time to go and visit Ma again. When they entered the room this time, she seemed to be breathing easier. Louie felt better.

"Go get something to eat," Ma said to Louie. "You'll like the food here. It's better than sardines and hard tack." She smiled at them both when they left the room.

"That's all we had to eat for days," Louie told Uncle Sam on their way to the cafeteria. "There was a woman named Evelyn with us there, and she complained every day." He quickly covered his mouth with his hands when he saw the person he had just named ahead of them in the cafeteria line.

"That's Captain Jack's—or Captain Spade's—I mean, that's his lady friend," stammered Louie. Evelyn heard Louie's voice and turned around. Before Louie could say anything else, she shook a fist at him and sneered, "You'll pay!"

When Uncle Sam and Louie had finished their meal and were back in the sitting room, Louie pulled out Charlie's letter from his pocket and showed it to Uncle Sam.

"I remember that funeral," Uncle Sam said. "There was something fishy about the way the captain wanted it to happen so soon after his ship returned. His poor son was still in shock."

"You mean Abram?" Louie asked. "He and I got to be good friends—even shared the same bed. He really misses his mother. He didn't like it when his papa invited Evelyn to go with them when he became captain of the *Sea Mist*—that was the name of the ship that wrecked. Abram thought that when his father invited him to go along during his Christmas vacation, it would be just him, his papa and the crew. But Evelyn came along. She and her fancy dresses! She never lifted a finger to help Ma, just complained all the time."

"Hmm," Uncle Sam said. "Maybe we should go and have a visit with this Captain Spade. If she's here in the hospital, he must be here, too."

# CHAPTER 26

# Visiting the Captain

U p those stairs and to the right," the receptionist answered when Uncle Sam asked for Captain Spade's room. "Room 26."

Louie stood beside Uncle Sam when he knocked on the door. "Come on in, mates," answered a male voice. Uncle Sam opened the door and the two walked in.

"Oh, it's you," said Captain Spade when he saw Louie. "Thought it was one of my crew. Doc Bowen tells me you helped save me." His leg—or what was left of it—was hoisted up on a sling. His hands were still bandaged.

"Lost the bottom of it," Captain Spade said when he saw Louie looking at the sling. "Guess I'll be called 'Peg Leg Jack.' Got some movement in my fingers, but the skin has to grow back—pretty painful at times."

"Do you remember me?" said Uncle Sam. He was now sitting down in a chair near the captain's bed. Louie held his cap in his hand and stood stiffly against the wall. There was a long silence, and then the captain looked down at his feet and answered, "Oh, yes. You did the funeral for my wife, Emily."

"Yes, your wife," replied Uncle Sam. "Louie tells me your wife visited Two Tree Island before you did."

"What? She couldn't have...wouldn't have..." Captain Spade caught himself before he finished his sentence.

"Wouldn't have survived, you mean?" said Uncle Sam.

Captain Jack's mouth opened.

"I didn't say she visited the island *alive*," continued Uncle Sam. "In fact, she was very much dead when her body arrived. All the morgue needs is for you to return and identify her."

Captain Jack's mouth closed, and purple spots appeared on his face. He shifted his body in the bed and looked away from Uncle Sam's piercing eyes.

"I remember you saying that you couldn't pay for your wife's funeral or burial—should her body be found," said Uncle Sam.

"Well, I can't pay now," snapped Captain Spade. "My ship with its load of sardines is gone because that boy let the lighthouse lamp go out." The captain's voice grew louder. "But he'll be forced to pay after the hearing," he snarled.

"Tell me the truth now, Captain Spade. How did your wife really die?" Uncle Sam got up to stand at the foot of the bed. Captain Spade's body became rigid and his features contorted.

"Nurse!" he yelled.

# CHAPTER 27

# Finding and Finishing

Louie and Uncle Sam left before the nurse arrived.

"You and I need to do some more investigating to collect as much information as we can concerning Captain Jack Spade," said Uncle Sam to Louie on their way down the stairs to the first floor. "I suspect his wife's death was no accident—if that woman's body is his wife. He'll probably want to delay being discharged from the hospital as long as possible so that he won't have to identify the body at the morgue. Now, don't you allow that man or his friend Evelyn to let you carry their guilt."

Three days later when Doc Bowen made his rounds, he declared Ma to be much improved. The tent had been taken away and she was sitting up in bed when Louie and Uncle Sam arrived. "Lungs sound good," Doc Bowen said to them as he placed his stethoscope around his neck. "Give her another week and she'll be good to go. Of course, she'll need to be careful for a while. Pneumonia leaves its mark and could return if she doesn't take care of herself."

"We'll make sure she does," said Louie and Uncle Sam in unison.

"About your examinations, Louie," Ma said after Doc Bowen had left the room. Now Louie knew she was better!

"I'm working on them, Ma," he said. Louie told her he had not been able to finish writing his book report without her help nor had he found the time to complete all his other assignments. "I'm not ready yet to take those exams," he added.

"Then I'm shooing both of you out of this hospital to get back to work and studying. I'll send for you when they're ready to let me go home."

Louie said goodbye to Uncle Sam, who promised to return when Doc Bowen released Ma from the hospital. They made a pact to talk to as many of Captain Spade's friends, associates and crew as possible.

"And Abram, too," added Louie. "I sure hope he doesn't have to see his mother's body to identify it."

"Don't worry," said Uncle Sam. " I'll go with him, if he's willing."

Louie boarded the *Rainbow* and within a short time was back at Two Tree Island. After the trauma of the shipwreck and Ma's illness, he found it hard to get back into his studies. But he had no other choice. Aussie and Harry had taken over most of his lighthouse chores and drilled him every night to prepare him for the examinations Miss Gilbert had sent.

When Louie had been back about a week, Gus brought a summons for him to appear at a hearing scheduled on February 22, just two weeks away. Mr. McAllister wrote in a letter accompanying the summons that he would dispatch a ship to come to Two Tree Island to escort Louie to the mainland on the day of the hearing. Mr. McAllister said he would also arrange for Mrs. Hollander to attend, if her health would permit. Louie could select two others to be his witnesses.

"Ayuh, lad, I'd be willin' to be yer witness," Harry said when Louie asked him at supper that night. "Don't ye worry, ye took good care of us. Dare say we can make a case for ye that it weren't yer fault we lost the *Sea Mist.*"

"What do you mean?" Louie asked. He then remembered about his agreement with Uncle Sam to find out as much information about Captain Jack Spade as he could.

"Well, Albert was at the wheel when yer light beacon flashed," Harry continued. "Captain had just come out on deck. Hadn't spent much time with us crew 'fore we sailed. He didn't know the name of the man on watch that hour, so he calls out, 'Who's on watch?' Then he yells, 'Who ever 'tis, turn sharp to starboard.' But Albert—not hearing his name—turned too late."

"What do you know about Captain Jack Spade?" Louie asked.

"Not much," Harry answered. "He was new to the ship, like most of the crew. He brought along Evelyn and his boy. We thought she was his wife, but Abram told me different. Douglas heard tell Captain likes the ladies and decks—not ship decks. Says he's seen him at them gambling places."

Louie cataloged this bit of information about Captain Spade in the back of his mind.

"Now about those examinations," Harry asked. "Are ye ready?"

"Just about," Louie replied.

# CHAPTER 28

# Time of Testing

B arnacles live in tide pools," Louie wrote in his natural history report. He chose these living creatures to write about because he had discovered so many of them attached to rocks and pieces of shell all around the perimeter of Two Tree Island.

"Wrongly classified as mollusks, they are a form of crustacean," he continued. "The barnacles we find on rocks are really the hard shells made of calcium carbonate by the cypris-like creatures inside. These crustaceans start as larvae. The larvae attach to hard surfaces with a sticky, glue-like substance. If they don't attach within 13 days, they die. The larvae live inside their shells in a watery substance when the tide is out. When the tide comes in again, they reach their tentacles out into the seawater through holes in their shells and grab tiny organisms floating by."

The weeks flew by as Louie studied and prepared for his examinations. Aussie helped him measure the various angles in his Fresnel lens drawing with a protractor and quizzed him about geometry terms. When Louie finished writing all his papers and reports and had studied until his brain was crammed so full of facts and figures it couldn't hold any more, he told Harry and Aussie that he was ready to take the examinations. Aussie and Harry took turns monitoring him. After Louie completed each of the examination papers, he put them in a large envelope to send to Miss Gilbert via Gus when Gus made his rounds of the islands.

Louie then convinced Harry and Aussie to allow him to help once again with lighthouse chores. "Well, we could use some help cleanin' windows in the tower and shoveling the walkways," said Harry.

While Louie was absorbed in his lessons, another blizzard had hit, piling up the snow in drifts around the house and lighthouse tower. During this winter storm, the three of them were able to spell each other to keep the fog siren going and the lamp lit. They had seen no ships around, but it had been difficult to get to Betsy and to keep the walkway to the tower cleared.

Louie busied himself posing Harry, Aussie and Scout for photographs with his new Brownie camera. Meanwhile, they waited for the weather to clear and either Gus's mail boat or the tender sent by Mr. McAllister to arrive.

# CHAPTER 29

# Countering Complaints

To him who is in fear, everything rustles." —*Sophocles*

The more time he had on his hands, the more Louie's fears about the upcoming hearing disturbed his thoughts. *Maybe the weather won't clear and the hearing will be delayed,* he thought. *Maybe Ma has gotten worse again. Maybe the Lighthouse Board will fire us. Maybe we'll have to pay for the ship that was wrecked. But how could we do that? Maybe we'll be sent to jail!*

Aussie noted the worry lines in Louie's face. "Scared, Louie?" he said.

Louie nodded and shuffled his feet.

"Don't do no good to let it eat at ye. Think about what ye know to be true."

"What's that?" Louie asked.

"Well, here's some facts to mull over," Harry said as he came in the door from the tower. "Yer ma was sick. The weather was bad. The ship could have been saved if the captain had paid more attention to knowing his crew. No one drowned. Besides, the weather just cleared, and I've seen a ship approaching."

Aussie looked through the spyglass. "Sure enough, looks like the lighthouse tender. You two better git ready."

Louie had already laid out the suit Ma had bought him for Charlie's pa's funeral. It took very little time to dress in the suit and pack the other items he would need in his duffel.

"Bye, Scout. Be good for Aussie," said Louie. He nuzzled his puppy before he caught up with Harry at the slip. Harry had already hauled up the dory. A sailor rowed the two of them out to the waiting tender, which covered the short distance to the town wharf in record time. When they arrived, they found a sleigh with two horses waiting to take them to the town hall where the hearing was to be held.

Louie's face beamed when he saw Uncle Sam come out of the door and down the steps to greet them at the town hall. "Your mother is already inside, Louie," he said. "She has been out of the hospital for a week and staying with the Bowlines. They're here, too, to support you."

Louie was surprised to see seated in the hearing room not only the Bowlines but also those whom he had met at clambakes and at Thanksgiving. Mr. McAllister sat with two other men dressed in lighthouse service uniforms at a table in the front of the room. Captain Spade sat in a wheelchair, and Evelyn and two other men sat on one side of the front of the room facing the table. Louie, Ma, Harry and a lawyer Uncle Sam introduced as Mr. Lewis were ushered to their seats on the other side.

Louie gave Ma a hug. "Be strong, son," she said. "Mr. Lewis will represent us well. Just answer his questions truthfully."

"This hearing is now in session," Mr. McAllister announced. "Mr. Jones, you may proceed."

One of the men on the other side of the room got up and spoke to the three officials at the table. "I represent Mr. Carlton, the owner of the *Sea Mist* and the Northeast Sardine Plant in Rockland. He is hereby filing a complaint against the keepers of Two Tree Island

Light hired by your board for causing the sinking of said ship. Because there was no light shining from the Lighthouse Tower the night of January 6, Mr. Carlton's ship hit a reef and sank off said island in Windlass Bay. My client, Mr. Carlton, along with Captain Spade, who was captaining the *Sea Mist* at the time she struck the reef, contend that the keepers of Two Tree Island Lighthouse, Molly Hollander and her son, Louie, are responsible for the loss of his fishing schooner. He seeks compensation for the total cost of his ship as well as the loss of revenue from the sardines in the hold that went down with the ship. I will call Evelyn, Mr. Carlton's daughter, who was on the ship at the time, as our first witness."

Louie noted that Abram was not anywhere in the room. Nor were the rest of the crew who had stayed with them.

Evelyn took a seat beside the table.

"Will you please tell the Board officials what happened the night of January 6?" Mr. Jones said to Evelyn.

"I was in the captain's quarters. . . with Jack," Evelyn began, "when I felt a shudder. Jack went out to see what was wrong. When he came back, he told me to come up on deck and get in the dory quickly. The ship was taking on water. I asked him to bring up my trunk first—my best clothes were in it—which he did while I dressed to be out in that cold weather. I don't like even to be on deck of a ship. One of the crew grabbed my arm and practically shoved me down the rope ladder so that I literally fell into the dory. I thought Jack would come, too, but Abram and two other seamen were already in the dory and there wasn't any room. Then we had to stay in their cramped house"—she pointed at Molly Hollander and Louie—"without any dry clothes and not enough food. My good clothes—the trunk did manage to float to shore—were ruined."

"Any other witnesses?" one of the officials seated at the table asked.

"Yes," replied Mr. Jones. "Captain Spade, please come forward and tell these officers what happened on the night of January 6."

Captain Spade moved his wheelchair forward and began. "We were on course for Rockland. We had eight barrels of sardines in the hold when a snow squall hit. I decided that with the weather taking a turn for the worse, we should head back to Rockland. Besides, we needed to get my son, Abram, back to school. I had gone below to retire for the night and left the crew in charge. I told them to follow the lighthouse beacons to find their way.

"I had just gone up on deck to check on the watch when I saw a light beacon dead ahead. I called to the man at the wheel to turn hard fast to starboard—but it was too late. The ship hit the reef and started taking on water. I ordered the dory lowered and got Evelyn, my son, Abram, Harry and Douglas over there and told them to row to shore. The other three of us made it to the stern and stood by the aft mast.

"Eventually, a hawser rope was sent out to us with a breeches buoy, and our cook and the last seaman got to shore. I stayed with the ship. Just before she sank, I saw the dory returning after delivering her passengers. I untied the rope around the mast and jumped overboard toward the dory. I held on to the rope and swam as best I could in the choppy sea until I lost consciousness.

"When I came around, I was in the house with my feet and hands bandaged. As you can see, I've lost part of a leg and a foot. As a sea captain, I depend on having the full use of my legs in order to captain a ship. I claim personal compensation for my loss."

"Thank you both," Mr. McAllister said. "You may return to your seats.

"Mr. Lewis, since you represent both Mrs. Hollander and her son Louie, would you like to state your defense?"

"Yes, thank you," said Mr. Lewis. "Mrs. Hollander has been in St. Mary's Hospital recuperating from a severe bout of pneumonia. We are grateful that she has recovered and is still with us."

The hearing room exploded with applause. Mr. McAllister pounded the table with a gavel.

"Silence! Please continue, Mr. Lewis."

"She apparently became ill shortly after Christmas day. She continued her duties as lighthouse keeper—taking turns with her son, Louie, during a blizzard to man the light beacon and fog siren—until she had no energy left and took to bed with a fever. Louie then took all the lighthouse shifts during the day and at night, while cooking the meals and taking care of his mother. On the night of January 6, he slept through and didn't trim the wick and fill the reservoir when it was time to do so. The lamp burned out.

"Mrs. Hollander says that when she awoke and realized the lamp was extinguished, she woke her son and the two of them went to the lighthouse tower to relight the lamp. When the Fresnel lens began to work again and the beacon started its round of illuminating the sea around Two Tree Island, they spotted the *Sea Mist* just before she hit the reef. They both went down to the landing site and were ready to launch their rescue dory when they saw that the ship's dory had already been launched. Louie directed the dory to shore with a lantern. Mrs. Hollander, who by this time was coughing badly, took that woman"—he pointed to where Evelyn was sitting—"back to the house while Louie got in the dory to go back out to the foundering ship to save our captain. No lives were lost as a result of his rescue efforts."

Mr. Lewis paused for a moment and then said, "I call Harry as our first witness."

After he had been sworn in, Harry took the seat next to the table and spoke. "This young man, Louie, is one of the bravest lads I've ever been privileged to meet."

Applause again broke out in the hearing room.

"Please," Mr. McAllister said. "Any more interruptions and you'll have to leave. Continue."

"He not only got the Lyle gun and hawser rope out for us crew to use, but he also risked his own life to save the captain. Not only did he lift him out of that frigid sea, but he also took off his own coat to cover him, gave him mouth-to-mouth resuscitation, and then lay on top of his cold, wet body until they reached shore. According to Doc Bowen, he saved the captain's life. He's a good lad, he is. Ain't no harm in falling asleep, especially since he had to take care of his ma and carry all the load of tending the lamp during a storm. Should give him a medal, you should."

"Objection!" Mr. Jones shouted.

"I ain't finished, yet," Harry continued. "Captain Jack here didn't know his crew by name—never even tried to learn their names. He spent most of his time in his cabin with *her*." He pointed to Evelyn. There was a gasp in the courtroom. "When he did come up that night, t'were too late."

"Any other witnesses, Mr. Lewis?" said Mr. McAllister.

"Yes, I'd like to call the young man, Louie Hollander, to testify."

Louie's knees knocked together. The palms of his hands started sweating. But Uncle Sam whispered, "You'll do fine, just answer Mr. Lewis's questions."

"Louie, I only have two questions," Mr. Lewis began. "How many days and nights did you have to tend the light beacon by yourself and take care of your mother?"

Louie thought for a moment and then answered, "I'd have to go back and look at the log book, sir, but I think it was about 12 days."

"And how many hours per night during that time did you sleep?"

"Not counting the night it happened…about two to three hours a night."

"That's all. You're excused."

Louie sat down and Uncle Sam rose. "Gentleman," he said, "I'd like to testify if I may. I know most of the folks around here because I am their summer pastor, and I've especially gotten to know this fine young man here." He nodded to Louie.

"All right," said Mr. McAllister. "You may do so, Reverend."

"I have taken the liberty to investigate Captain Jack Spade, because I became suspicious when he asked me to conduct his wife's funeral after his last trip at sea…"

"Irrelevant! Objection!" shouted Mr. Jones.

"I think you will find, gentlemen, if you allow me to finish what I have to tell you, that what I found out in my investigation is very relevant."

The officers at the table nodded, and one of them said, "Considering what Harry has told us, we'd like to hear what you did find in your investigation. Please continue."

"First, I searched out the crew of the ship that Captain Spade skippered before he got the job on the *Sea Mist* and interviewed two of the seamen. Captain Spade had told me that his wife, who had accompanied him on his prior voyage, had been washed out to sea by a rogue wave and that her body disappeared. Well, when I interviewed these crew members—and I have their testimonies here"—he laid some papers on the table—"they told me there had been no rogue wave, but that one morning they woke and the lady had just disappeared. The captain said she was too sick to come up on deck, but they didn't see her get off the ship."

All eyes and ears were now on Uncle Sam. "After I had these men write down their testimonies, I decided to ask around town to find out if anyone else knew the captain and his family. I found out two interesting pieces of information. Captain Spade's son, Abram, spent most of his time living with an aunt and his mother while the captain was at sea or in one of the gambling places around. Apparently, the captain owed some sizable debts. I also went with Abram to see if he could recognize the woman's body at the morgue that Louie found on Two Tree Island last fall. Even though the body was beyond recognition, Abram was able to identify a piece of jewelry found by Lt. Gillespie, the life-saving inspector, that he had seen his mother wear."

The observers in the hearing room gasped. Captain Spade scowled at Mr. Jones, who tried to raise an objection. Mr. McAllister pounded the gavel and said that the hearing board would meet to decide what action to take on the complaints for compensation before them. He asked all the concerned parties to return the next morning. "And none of you leave town," he added.

Louie walked out of the room with Ma on one side and Uncle Sam and Harry on the other. Cries of "you're welcome to stay with us!" and "come join us for supper!" greeted them outside. A reporter stepped in front of Louie.

# CHAPTER 30

# Conclusion

"What was it like finding her body?" the reporter asked. The reporter took out a writing pad and pencil and began to take notes as Louie answered.

"My dog, Scout, really found the body. At first, I just thought it was some flotsam that had floated in on the tide. However, when I tried to drag it onto land, I saw these eyes and went to fetch Ma. We covered the body and put out an SOS."

Louie, Ma, Harry and Uncle Sam managed to escape the rest of the reporter's questions and squeeze into a waiting carriage that took them back to the Bowlines.

"I'm proud of you, Louie, for holding your own," Ma said after they were safely inside the Bowline house.

"Glad you did yer own investigation," Harry said to Uncle Sam.

"Puts that sleazy captain on the defensive instead of these fine folk," replied Uncle Sam.

"How did Abram take seeing the body of his mother?" Louie asked.

"He was broken up, but his aunt is taking good care of him. He's rehearsing for his role in *Huck Finn*. Maybe I can take you and your mother back with me to watch the performance."

"But I need to get back to tend the light," Ma said.

"Well, ma'am," Harry said, "I'm not goin' nowhere for the rest of the winter. Aussie and I can manage. Why, you and Louie here deserve a break. Go ahead and go with the good Rev'rend."

"We promised to take good care of you, remember?" said Uncle Sam as he grinned at Louie. "Besides, this lonely bachelor could use some company."

"And I've just taken my exams and am caught up with all my lessons," Louie added.

Ma finally relented, and all agreed that as soon as the hearing ended, with Mr. McAllister's permission, Louie and Ma would return to stay with Uncle Sam. The next morning, Louie and Ma were seated in the hearing room when Mr. McAllister and the other officials entered. The townsfolk they knew were already seated in the available chairs. Others stood against the walls.

"We have come to a consensus," said Mr. McAllister. "In the matter of the complaint filed by Mr. Carlton and Captain Spade that Louie Hollander and Mrs. Hollander caused the recent sinking of the *Sea Mist*, we find the defendants not guilty."

A cheer went up in the room. Mr. McAllister had to pound the gavel several times before the room came to order and he could continue.

"In fact, we commend Louie Hollander for his heroism in rescuing Captain Spade and for manning the light during his mother's serious illness. Now, in regard to the issues of compensation requested: Captain Spade's disability compensation and compensation to Mr. Carlton for the loss of the *Sea Mist* and subsequent loss of revenue for the sardine company. While it is true that the Lighthouse Board has been commissioned by the United States Congress to build and outfit lighthouse stations to help our maritime fleet identify dangerous reefs and to hire keepers to man the lamps and sirens on those stations, the board is not responsible for acts of nature or the negligence of ship captains."

Another cheer came from the listening crowd of onlookers.

"Please," Mr. McAllister pleaded, "wait until we conclude the hearing before you interrupt me one more time." He banged the gavel and continued.

"Furthermore, the Lighthouse Board has positioned lighthouses along this particular coast at equal distances so each ship captain should be able to plot a course to a destinatione as well as avoid dangerous reefs, regardless of whether or not a lighthouse is functioning. Fishing and canning companies take an added risk when they send a fishing ship out to fish during the fall and winter months when severe storms are likely to occur. So the risk of loss is on them, not on the Lighthouse Board or the keepers the board hires."

Mr. Jones rose to object and challenge the board findings, but Mr. McAllister immediately silenced him. "Mr. Jones, I think you would do well to sit down and consult Captain Spade about retaining you to be his defense attorney. I have wired the police department in Rockland. Based on the testimony we have heard, I have recommended that they arrest Captain Spade on charges of murder in the matter of his wife's death. This hearing has now ended."

**Pleasant
Word**

To order additional copies of this title call:
1-877-421-READ (7323)
or please visit our web site at
www.pleasantwordbooks.com

If you enjoyed this quality custom published book,
drop by our web site for more books and information.

www.winepressgroup.com

"Your partner in custom publishing."

Printed in the United States
200294BV00005B/22-72/A